DevilMENt

FOR LITERARY HEAT

www.BarbarianSpy.com

WARNING: This book is for sale to **ADULT AUDIENCES ONLY**. Contains graphic gay male sex, reluctance, multiple partners, anal sex, nongraphic violence, and the devil, all of which may be considered offensive by some readers.

All sexually active characters in this work are at least 18 years of age.

BarbarianSpy
Jindalee St
Toronto, NSW 2283

DevilMENt

A Devilish Collection

from

habu

Table of Contents

Introduction

What would the hallowing season of the year be without a bit of devilment? In these ten short stories, the devil appears—or doesn't appear or, scary thought, appears to not be the most evil force that can visit earth. And he comes in all, or at least some aspect, of his glory—not only as a separate form, but sometimes from within the human characters themselves.

The young male protagonists of these stories learn not only what a deal with the devil can get you but also what selling your soul entails. Many (but not all) of these strapping young men find that it's a more tolerable, pleasurable even, price than they had imagined—if only for a short time.

In "Soul Bait," the devil delves into the world of Internet porn and its allure to trap men's souls. The story, "So You Want to Be in Movies," is a "the devil made me do it" approach to entering the film industry through porn films. "Imagine" delves into the horror side of devilment as the relationship between two step-brothers sinks into madness. The fourth story in the collection warns envious young men to take a careful look at deals being offered with a "Devilish Grin." As "The Devil Made Me Do

It" illustrates, if you haze someone bad enough, the devil is on call for revenge.

The second half of the anthology takes us on a desert rally in northern Africa in "Cure of the Tan Tan" for a truly horrific devilish experience. Whereas an earlier story in the collection ("Devilish Grin") was constructed around the devil using a young man's envy to trap him, "Paulo's Inferno" is a historical piece, taking us back to Italy at the advent of automobiles, for the devil to use ambition to capture a young man's soul. "Beat the Devil" is a fantasy story of forces of the devil fighting for control of an alpine German village. The devil of "Shark" is a slick con man in a metallic blue Corvette convertible, preying on bored young men in farming communities. The last story in the collection, "Demon Spiral," shows how little indiscretions can blossom into big trouble—with a little demonic help.

The devil comes in many forms, both externally and internally, but everything devilish in *DevilMENt* comes with the purpose to possess young men's bodies—and their souls—fully.

Soul Bait

The young man sat at the sidewalk café in Fairfax City near George Mason University in the Virginia suburbs of Washington, D.C., sipping coffee and shyly looking around him. Several tables away from him and behind him sat a somewhat older man, perhaps in his forties, but very good looking in a dark, foxy sort of way. This man also was drinking coffee and looking around. But he was more assured in his demeanor and spent much of his time watching the younger man.

The younger man was a strikingly good-looking blond—one who many other patrons of the café, which specialized in gay college students from the nearby university, would call twinky, cute, almost beautiful, his features combined, pale blue eyes; long, dark eyelashes; a shy smile; and sensuous lips. The overall impression was soft, almost feminine. He didn't have feminine mannerisms, though. It was more that he was shy and unsure of himself in this environment.

In this venue, though, he was a man magnet. Some professor types and a few more athletic types from the university and even some cruising businessmen from across northern Virginia were circling around the table where he sat—a two-seat table—like bees shopping for pollen. Several of them asked if the other seat at his table was taken in the time that the man sitting behind him observed his actions—this despite there being more than enough tables available in mid afternoon. But each time the young man hesitated and eventually said that he was sorry but that he was expecting someone.

After an hour's observation, the dark presence behind him, Darien, decided that the one the young man was waiting for was someone named courage. He concluded that the young man knew what he sought but didn't have the courage to accept what was offered. This even though the men asking if he wanted company universally were very well put together.

At length the young man pulled something from the leather portfolio that had been sitting on the table top, rose, and walked over to a notice board that the café kept near the entrance to the indoor section of the café. He posted a notice on the board, looked around, and then left the café. On his way out, a college jock type black guy reached out with a beefy hand and arrested the young man's progress by touching his forearm. They talked briefly. Darien watched closely, thinking that, at last, a hookup had been made and that the two young men would leave together. But the young blond, blushing, pulled away and hurriedly left the café.

When the young man was gone, Darien rose from his table and walked over to the notice board. He had watched carefully to see what the young man had posted there and quickly located it. It was one of those "service's offered" notices, made on a computer, and had separated strips of paper along the bottom that gave a telephone number. There was an address on the notice. Darien took the notice off the board, folded it, and put it in his pocket.

He wouldn't keep it, he thought. He was just borrowing it for a couple of days—so that his would be the first response.

Darien left the café and got into his black Porsche Boxster convertible in time to see the young man, in a light blue Corolla sedan, pull out of a parking space and head east on Old Lee Highway, Route 29, toward the Capitol Beltway that circled the nation's capital.

Darien followed the Corolla at a distance. He had the address printed on the notice, but he wanted to see what kind of place it was. The young man stopped, once, at a small grocery store inside the beltway. Darien was heartened at the evidence that the one plastic bag the young man came out of the store with indicated the young man was cooking for just one.

Darien pulled up to the curb on a shaded, tree-lined, long-established residential street of Falls Church, a Revolutionary War-era town that had been swallowed up by the near suburbs of Washington, D.C. The houses now in this area mostly weren't large and were built in the styles of the late 1950s and early 1960s, when the federal bureaucracy at the center was burgeoning and the need for expansion in Washington's bedroom communities in Virginia and Maryland was pressing. The houses were mostly of mellow red brick, and most of them were enclosed in billowing azalea bushes and were well maintained—in keeping with their current value of more than half a million dollars each because of location, location, location.

The house that the young man stopped at was a split foyer. The portico porch was set half way between the first and second floor and the first floor was buried up to the bottom of its windows in the ground. The lots along the street slopped to the rear so that even the basements of the one-story ramblers were "walk-out" at the rear.

The young man pulled into a parking apron wide enough for two cars that was set off in front of the split foyer and walked up to the front door of the house. He used keys in two locks to enter the house and, Darien could tell, went down to the lower level, because twilight was setting in and lights were turned on on that level.

Darien gave a tight little smile and drove off slowly. Chances were very good, he thought, that he had found his bait. The young guy had shown in the café that he was a man magnet.

* * * *

"How old did you say you were?"

Andrew Temple hadn't said how old he was, but he was polite by nature and more than a bit nervous, so he answered. "I'm twenty-two."

Darien wasn't blessed with politeness, but the young man had something he wanted, so he, in turn, didn't say what he was

11

thinking—that Andrew Temple didn't look nearly as old as twenty-two. This too, though, fell in with Darien's intentions. "It's just that this is a very nice house in a very nice neighborhood. It seems strange that one so young owned it. You do own it, don't you?"

"Yes, yes, it's mine. I inherited it. We moved here my third year in high school. My mother and me. My father had died. My mother wasn't well, though. My parents had me late in life. Soon after we moved in, my mother became an invalid and spent much of her time upstairs. There's a full layout upstairs. Three bedrooms and two baths. A nice living room, dining room, kitchen and family room made out of a screened porch on the back of the house. I wouldn't rent to more than two, so each could have a bath of his own and there'd be a guest room the two could split the use of. Would you like to see it now?"

"Later," Darien answered. "I'd like to listen to you now. So it's the upstairs you want to rent rooms in?"

He was leaning over the coffee table, giving the young man his full attention. This both gratified and rattled Andrew. He was used to people trying to get close to him—naturally drawn to him—but he usually avoided being alone with anyone else because he was so self-conscious and torn by what he wanted—and afraid of how easily he was aroused by handsome, fit, self-confident men. And Darien was all of that, in a dark, mysterious, dangerous sort of way. Darien was everything that aroused Andrew in his isolated little world. This was the stuff of his dreams, but now that the man was here, in his living room—on the ground floor of the house—Andrew was trembling with nerves.

"Yes . . . yes, the upstairs. I have a complete apartment down here."

"Complete with your own bedroom?"

"Yes," Andrew answered. It came out with almost a hiccup, though, and a shudder. The man had his arms in front of him, his long, sensuous fingers making little patterns on top of the coffee table, mere inches from Andrew's knees, which, through no will of Andrew's own, were moving even closer to his side of the coffee table. His legs involuntarily spread in reaction to the tightening feeling in his groin. He needed more room in the basket of his briefs.

"I, uh . . . need to rent out a couple of rooms, because, although I own the house, there are larger expenses than I can manage on my own. The utilities and the property taxes are high. And maintenance on a house this old . . . but I'm being a bad host. I haven't even offered you anything to drink. Would you like coffee, water, or tea . . . or beer?" He struggled to his feet. Trembling more when he realized that the tenting of his trousers clearly showed that he was hard—and Darien was making no effort to show he was looking anywhere but at Andrew's basket.

"Anything is fine with me. Water is good. You can't hack the expenses of this house on your own? Are you still a student?"

"Yes. I'm going to George Mason. But only part time. I'm working as an editor for a publisher too. Children's books."

Darien laughed. It wasn't really a pleasant laugh, and it made Andrew blush. He couldn't see anything wrong in editing children's books and wondered what Darien had against that. But the fox-like man dispelled the notion that he disapproved.

"Perfect. Children's books. That's just perfect. So, I found your notice at a café near George Mason. Is that who you wanted to answer the ad—just more young men college students? I'm too old?"

"No, of course you're not too old, if you are interested in a room. You're the only one to contact me as yet," Andrew answered, flustered at the challenge. He knew that Darien had gotten his number from the notice put up at the gay café in Fairfax City. It's the only place Andrew had posted the notice. He kept fighting with himself about posting elsewhere, but his need—coming out of him despite all of his trepidation and reticence—had been to have someone come live here, with him—someone who could become more than just a tenant.

Andrew wasn't a virgin to men—well, to one man. One of his professors at George Mason his first year had seduced him and they'd been together whenever they could without Andrew's mother knowing about it. They even had made love here in the house but had to be very quiet about it. Andrew had had plans for after his mother died. He didn't really want her to die. He very much was a momma's boy. But her dying was inevitable. The irony had been that the professor had died first.

There had been no replacement, although Andrew pined to have a man between his legs. He had been the one seduced, though, and the professor had done all of the controlling. Andrew didn't have the courage to make the moves himself—even though men gravitated to him wherever he went. He could have hooked up at the café the other day when he put the notice up. Several men tried to sit with him. The black jock, when he was leaving, had been very explicit about what he wanted. Andrew wanted it too. He just had trouble going over that edge.

"I'll be right back with the drinks," he said, flustered, as he came around the coffee table and headed toward his small kitchenette. He half hoped that the man, Darien, would reach out for him with those hands with the long, sensuous fingers as he passed by, but Darien just gave him a hooded, sexy look with his eyes.

When Andrew came back with two glasses of ice water in hand, he found that Darien had moved over to the sofa. Andrew put the two glasses down on the coffee table. He was jostling both and water was spilling out. He reached over the table for a paper napkin to use to wipe up the spill as he prepared to sit in the chair across the table from the sofa Darien had vacated. But Darien reached out with a hand and took Andrew's wrist.

"You're trembling. Don't be afraid. Here, leave that and sit next to me." The fingers of Darien's hand were searing hot on Andrew's wrist, and he had the sensation that he needed to break away now and go to the stairs up to the foyer and escape the house. Now. But he didn't. He also realized that ever since the black jock had touched his arm at the café, he wanted to be led away and fucked by a man. He docilely walked around the side of the coffee table and sat down close beside Darien.

Andrew both knew what was coming next and rejected in his mind that it could possibly happen.

Darien put one arm around Andrew's shoulders, pulling him in, and moved the other hand to his lap, covering Andrew's erection.

"Please. What are you—?"

"Just relax, Andrew, I'm going to fuck you." Darien's voice was smooth, almost sing song, the calmness and naturalness of the tone belying the message he voiced. He made it sound so reasonable. "I know it's what you want. You put that notice up in a gay café. I know what sort of man you wanted to answer the ad. And I'm the one who came. You've wanted me to fuck you since you let me in the house."

Andrew began to mew his objections, but Darien had a grip on the hair at the back of his head, pulled his head back, and came down from on top with his face to possess Andrew's mouth with his. Even the kiss was reassuring and made it all seem so natural. If someone's saliva could be said to be a sedative drug, Darien's was. While they kissed, Darien unzipped Andrew's trousers, pulled out his hard cock, and began to stroke him. As he stroked and held Andrew in the kiss, the young man began to relax into soft moans and "whatever you want" responses.

This was the groove Andrew was used to—that his old professor had dominated him with. All of the decisions and actions were shouldered by the other man.

This indeed was what he'd dreamed about—and thought about at night all the time he was developing a plan to bring men into his home. But this was so much more of a fulfillment of what he'd hoped or that he'd had any idea he could get. He knew it was too much and happening too fast, but a great lethargy was cloaking him, and he just gave Darien anything he wanted.

Darien wanted it all. And Darien wanted it now.

Andrew lay back into the sofa as Darien undressed him and then, standing in front of Andrew, undressed himself. Throughout Darien managed to keep and hand—or even just fingers—touching Andrew, and this was all it took to hold the young man in thrall.

Darien was both lithe and well-muscled. A perfect male body. His cock and balls, though, hung so low that the promise of them made Andrew whimper in fear—and there was a thick silver ring in the head of the cock. An intricate tattoo of some sort of mythical creature—a dragon for something, in shades of red, was inked to appear to be draped on Darien's left shoulder, with a paw with sharp claws coming around his neck, the other forepaw appearing under his left arm pit at his side, and the two lower legs hooked on his waist on either side just above where Darien's hip bone flared out. The head of the dragon, with flicking tongue and piercing eyes came down from Darien's left shoulder. The creature was staring menacingly at Andrew, ready to pounce at any instant.

Andrew didn't even realize that Darien was standing on the sofa, with his feet on either side of Darien's thighs and feeding his cock into Andrew's mouth, until Andrew experienced the feel of the cock ring clicking against his teeth as Darien held his head on both sides and guided it in a face fuck.

The next thing Andrew knew was that he was draped along the sofa, with his chest on an arm, and his head and arms dangling over the side down to the floor. Darien ate his ass out and then mounted him and fucked him slowly, deeply, interminably. It wasn't a rough fuck. It was a sensuous, moaning total exploration of Andrew's ass canal with the rubbing of the cock ring. It was only when Darien ejaculated in four long flows that Andrew discovered he wasn't wearing a condom. And Andrew was so mellow that he didn't care.

The cum had a sedative effect on Andrew, and he gave himself up completely to whatever Darien wanted to do with him.

As much cum as Darien had produced, though, he wasn't finished, He lifted Andrew in his arms—Andrew being of slight stature and Darien having surprising strength for a slender figure—and carried the cute young blond into one of the two bedrooms—obviously the master bedroom—that were on this level. There he fucked Andrew again, in the missionary position, on the bed. Andrew loved every stroke of it, which continued beyond both of their ejaculations and put Andrew into a mellow doze.

He woke to Darien coming out of the adjoining bathroom, toweling himself off after a shower.

"My luggage is in the car. You can bring it in."

"But I haven't shown you the upstairs yet," Andrew answered, his voice sounding far away even to himself.

"I will be sleeping down here. In the other bedroom down here—when I'm not fucking you. You'll still have two rooms to rent upstairs then. After you've brought my luggage in, you should fix us some supper. I'm quite hungry."

All of this sounded quite reasonable to Andrew. He did Darien's bidding without question. After dinner, he sat curled up in the chair on the other side of the sofa and watched Darien working in his laptop computer. It wasn't Darien's laptop; it was Andrew's. And none of this now seemed strange to Andrew. He hadn't even given it a thought when he lifted the two untouched glasses of water from the coffee table top and saw that the rings the glasses left overlapped. That was scientifically impossible, but Andrew was able to accept anything involving Darien now.

That was a good thing, because Darien—or what Darien became—fucked Andrew throughout the night on Andrew's bed.

They started out in a lotus position, facing each other, Andrew's thighs over Darien's, Darien's cock buried inside Andrew's passage, and Darien gripping Andrew's waist. Andrew moaned and sighed and murmured of his complete taking, as Darien's already long and thick cock lengthened and thickened cock progressive grew as it slid up, through Andrew's intestines toward his stomach.

Andrew arched back in Darien's grip and swayed side to side and forward and back as he watched the lighting in the room go blood red, Darien's own body reddened as well, small horns budded out at Darien's temples, the dragon started to undulate on Darien's back, and the tail of something—the dragon? Darien?—thumped on the surface of the bed behind Darien as he mined Andrew's intestines ever deeper, releasing cum periodically. Each release of cum reassured Andrew even more that everything was right with the world and that this was exactly what he wanted.

Andrew arched all the way back, arms thrown over his head, forearms dangling toward the floor, as Darien, knees pressed in under Andrew's buttocks, wishboned Andrew's legs straight out from his hips, and dug deeper with the snake of his cock. Andrew reasoned that it was just an illusion that the bulb of Darien's cock was pressing at the back of his tonsils—even when Darien's body jerked and cum burbled out of Andrew's month and dribbled down his chin.

* * * *

The next morning, Darien made Andrew rewrite his ad for the bedrooms upstairs. Taking what Andrew wrote earlier and that had been taken off the board at the gay café by Darien right after Andrew had posted it, Darien had him add some detail. Now

Andrew was looking for a male graduate student working part time, who had Christian values, and his own laptop—which had to be shown to Andrew upon interviewing for the room. The price was set ridiculously low and Darien had Andrew append a photo of himself in gym clothes to the ad. The only thing Andrew asked about was the laptop requirement, to which Darien said that surely he didn't want someone who would be always asking someone else to lend him their computer.

This made sense to Andrew. Just about everything Darien said to him or asked him to do made sense to Andrew. And anything that didn't Andrew would stifle just for a total fuck by Darien like he'd had the night before.

After giving Andrew a nice little fuck and leaving him on the bed moaning and not being able to close his legs, Darien drove back to the gay café in Fairfax City and posted the new version of the ad. Once again, it had separated tabs at the bottom with Andrew's phone number on it.

And, as before, the gay café was the only place the ad was posted.

The first young man to answer the ad wasn't a graduate student, nor did he have a part-time job. But he was senior at George Mason, the captain of the basketball team, and the head of the university's Christian Union. Both Andrew and Darien were there when the young man arrived. Darien took the laptop and went off in the other room long enough for Andrew's natural charm along with the sexual luster Darien had given him to work magic on Austen, the basketball player, enough for Andrew soon to be on all fours on the living room carpet and Austen to be covering him from on top and riding the young blond's ass with his cock.

The Web site addition made on Austen's computer, Darien returned to the room and watched until Austen had gotten his rocks off and Andrew had told him he could have one of the rooms upstairs. Then Andrew sat and watched in awe as Darien expertly seduced the basketball player into accepting cock as well and fucked him in the same position on all fours on the living room floor that Austen had just used to fuck Andrew.

That night, in one of the bedrooms upstairs, Darien gave Austen the full-night, devilish fuck, and thereafter Austen was as docile for him as Andrew was. Austen remained randy for Andrew and received privileges in that way.

After another day, though, Andrew had to schedule these privileges. At Darien's direction, because he said he needed a full day to "process" an applicant, Andrew didn't schedule more than one interview for the room each day, but by the end of the next day he had his second tenant.

The next applicant to appear wasn't a student. Daniel was a teacher at a Christian high school. And he was married, he admitted, but he was looking for a more private room he could call his own. He obviously also was looking for a young man to fuck. He fucked Andrew while Andrew sat in his lap on the sofa and Darien fiddled with the man's computer before he easily seduced and fucked him in the same manner, and tucked him away in the second bedroom upstairs, where, that night, he gave the early thirtyish teacher the devilish treatment while Austen fucked Andrew in Andrew's bedroom.

Darien gave the opinion that Andrew could let all three bedrooms upstairs and just cut the rent a bit on the two who would have to share the hall bath. Andrew just nodded his head in agreement.

The third applicant was a bust. He not only wasn't a student working part time but he also had no connection to Christian organizations. He was a businessman who, though young and quite good looking, was not what Darien was looking for. He owned a Victoria's Secret store and took his jollies close to his work. He wore ladies' lingerie and was querying whether Andrew would be willing to wear panties and a bra while they fucked too. Andrew was willing. Darien had made him highly randy and ready for about anything—and the lingerie salesman was quite a hunk. Darien had been in the kitchenette working on the man's computer when he overheard this conversation, though. He called Andrew on his cell phone from the kitchen, asked him to come talk to him for a few minutes, and when Andrew returned to the living room, he had to suggest that the businessman put his clothes back on and regretfully informed him that the call was from someone already interviewed who was prepared to say he wanted the last remaining bedroom upstairs.

The next day, the ensemble was made complete. Michael, a Caucasian-Chinese mix, not only was a part-time student at George Mason, but he also was the youth counselor in a large evangelical church in Fairfax City.

He had answered a rather explicit ad posted at a gay café, though.

Darien thought he was perfect, and he enjoyed working on Michael's computer, favoriting several interesting pornographic Web sites for Michael. Andrew thought that Michael's missionary fuck position was perfect, Michael thought that Darien's missionary fuck position was even better, and Darien gave Michael the devil treatment throughout that night in the third bedroom upstairs while Austin, Daniel, and Andrew engaged in a threesome in Andrew's bedroom.

The last day Darien was there he spent using his wiles to increase Austen's, Daniel's, and Michael's hots for Andrew and for playing with the nifty Web site and files Darien had added to their computers. While Darien fiddled with the computers, Andrew reveled in swimming in the cum of the three up to his eyeballs. Darien also used his charms to largely erase himself from the memories of all four young men, so that when he drove away from the house for the last time, the others didn't really remember he'd been there. They just knew they had found sexual nirvana—both in reality with the young and cute blond, Andrew, and with the delights Darien had embedded in their computers.

Darien only had to sit through two days of surreptitious surveillance of Andrew's house from down the block while sitting in his Porsche Boxster for the efficiency of the Fairfax City police to take hold, in the form of the cyber police squad knocking on Andrew's door.

Just under ten days and four souls gathered, including Andrew's, who had been the bait. Five, if the Victoria's Secret businessman was tracked down as well. Not a bad take, Darien thought. But the challenge was always there to do better. His record had been in Las Vegas, but that was hardly fair to count, Las Vegas being Las Vegas.

So You Want to Be in Movies

"So, my agent said it was for some sort of commercials for the Halloween season."

"Yes, that's right. It's for commercial use to be released a few weeks before Halloween, yes."

I needed the work. The plays on Broadway were shutting down almost as fast as they opened. It was just bad luck, a bunch of new plays that weren't piquing the audience's interest and some tired old revivals. There was more creative work being done off Broadway and in some clubs. I liked doing those, but they didn't pay too well. I was barely getting by.

"I've looked at a bunch of résumés that were sent to me by the New York agents, and yours was one of the standouts. Good enough for us to pay your way down here."

"Yes, I was surprised to get a call from here. New York isn't exactly—"

"New York has a freer environment overall. It's where our best talent comes from."

I didn't want to argue myself out of a possible gig, so I didn't pursue that point. The pay would be good. Real, real good for the number of hours it should entail. And commercials. They were great exposure for guys trying to break into movies. Which was what I was trying to do. Me and thousands of other young, good-looking guys, I'd found. But I had talent. I'd been in two Broadway plays, one with a small speaking part. If either one had lasted more than two weeks, I would have been sitting pretty. And I was doing OK in Off Broadway and in the private clubs. Of course, the sooner I could get out of the private clubs, the better.

We were sitting in the out-door section of a café above the Virginia Beach boardwalk, and I was dividing my time between listening to the Holland guy and watching a volleyball game going on between muscle studs in their tiny Speedos below us. These obviously were guys more there to be seen than to play volleyball.

Andrew Holland was quite a looker too. He was the film producer who had paid my way down here. I was looking past him at the table down at the volleyball players and there wasn't much difference between him and them other than age—and I wasn't at all sure I didn't give him the edge on desirability.

He was the mature Paul Newman type—with watery blue eyes, good facials, and silver gray hair, which, on him, as was the case occasionally, made him look younger than a guy should be with a full head of gray hair. He had a nice smile, and I liked that he was keeping this interview balanced—selling me on his project as much as testing me for suitability for the gig. He had a smooth and easy delivery. A perfect salesman type, but one of million-dollar projects, not used Edsels. He also, from what I could see, was as cut—especially for his age—as any of the young guys at the volleyball net. He was wearing a silver-gray-colored sports coat, but under that was a form-fitting black polo shirt. It all went perfectly well with the watery blue eyes, open smile, and perfectly cut gray hair.

The only incongruity I noticed, and I had no idea how to even ask about it, was that he was wearing close-fitting black-leather gloves. It didn't seem to limit the dexterity of his hands, though. There had been no hesitation or awkwardness in picking up his beer glass. He seemed completely at home in the gloves. But I kept looking at those gloves as he talked.

I had no idea how I had gotten there. I was bound, naked, in a spread X, on my back, on a bondage table, my mouth gagged with a ball gag. A man in a devil's mask and black cape, but otherwise naked except for black-leather gloves and a studded chest harness, was standing next to the table, hovering over me, slowly stroking my cock. His build was mature and I could see the gray hair above the devil's mask, but his body was trim and well-muscled.

He was hard, and what he was swinging was nothing to laugh at. I was already hard too and was raising my pelvis to the jacking, curling my trapped fingers and toes, and pulling hard at the bonds. Wanting to be free, but not for escape anymore. No, I wanted to do more in the sexual encounter.

His stroking, going off beat now and then to make me shudder, was driving me crazy. Relentlessly stroking me, sending me high above the clouds. I came, but he didn't stop stroking. He slowed down from the crescendo he'd reached, but he didn't stop. It was painful at first, and I begged in muffled sounds through the gag for relief, but he didn't stop, bringing me hard again and then to another ejaculation. Pulling on my cock with that gloved hand. No sense of the passage of time, knowing only that he had been at it for a long time. Starting for a third time . . .

He was mounting the bondage table, straddling my chest. He freed me of the ball gag, cupped my head in his hands, and presented his hard cock for sucking. The pubic hair nesting his cock was black with streaks of gray. Curly; smelt of musk. My chance to participate more in the sexual encounter.

". . . specialty films, really."

My attention came back to the present. Holland was leaning over the table, deeper into a sales pitch. It wasn't a pitch he needed to give me. He had me at the fee quote—and the anticipation that it would be shown on TV. Commercials. Advertising I didn't have to pay for, one way or the other. And in New York, payment in the entertainment world didn't always come in the form of cash. If he wanted me to get up from this table and go with him to nail down the audition, I was prepared to go. I can't say I didn't want to go.

In the New York world, he'd said.

"Why Virginia Beach, down in Virginia?" I asked, not even aware of why I asked, but needing to get back into the conversation, needing not to reveal that I had been off into a

23

disturbing fantasy. I was trying to keep my eyes off the tight-fitting black gloves. I thought that it would make him mad for me to draw attention them. But he was expressive when he talked. They were waving in front of my face. There was no way I could avoid looking at them.

"The Navy mostly—and production costs. Lots of naval presence here, and it's actually cheaper to bring whoever we need down from New York or out from Los Angeles than to pay the New York or California production prices."

Los Angeles. I ached to be in Los Angeles. In movies.

"The Navy? You do training films?"

"Yes, we do a lot of training films. Navy guys are naturals for that. That's sort of what this film is about too. Demonstrating how the technique we're showing is done."

My attention was arrested by the volleyball game down on the beach. It had been disbanded. There were still two studly looking guys down there, though. One was backed up against a light pole at the edge of the sand, his arms drawn above his head and his fists clutching the stem of the pole above him. The other guy was leaning close in to him with a hand on his waist, speaking low and seemingly intensely to the other guy. I was projecting the kiss—and was both titillated and surprised at the image occurring right out here on the open public beach.

But they just stood there for a while and then both turned and walked off. They walked close together, though, the one guy's arm around the waist of the other guy, holding him in close to the hip and giving the impression of having full control. Climbing the steps, walking to the entrance to the ocean-side lobby of the hotel next to where we were sitting. The two guys turned their eyes to each other. The face I could see was of the guy being led. There were mixed signals there, I thought. He turned back toward the ocean front at the door, almost as if he was going to pull back, walk away. There were two hands on his waist now, though, turning him back to the Hotel entrance, gently pushing him inside.

I was bound wrists and ankles, standing facing and bound to a Saint Andrew's cross inside a room painted all in black. I was looking at a full-length mirror mounted on the wall across the room, so I could watch it all. I could see a mound of black material through the bottom of the legs of the cross that my legs were spread and bound to. The material spilled out around the edges of the cross limbs. It was moving, undulating, in a rhythm that I could feel all the way through my naked body. My cock had been pulled between my legs and was being sucked by an expert mouth—a mouth and throat that could take me deep and hold me inside, throbbing. Keep me gasping for breath.

A hand laced my balls between its leather-covered fingers, pulling them out from my body and squeezing and rolling them. I got the full effect of my facial expressions through the V of the top of the cross—my mouth open and slack, my eyes slitted in combined pain and ecstasy. Breathing heavy, panting. I could clearly hear my own moans. My cock was free except that the hand worrying my balls had moved a gloved finger to encase the root of the staff. My entrance was being rimmed and flicked with a tongue. The tongue was pressing inside. The finger encircling the base of my cock tightened its squeeze. My balls were being rolled and pulled.

I could hear a voice murmuring weakly, "Fuck me. Please fuck me now." I only belatedly realized that it was my own voice.

And the answering laugh. I could not get the raspy answering laugh out of my mind.

When I had come, the figure rose behind me, and the mask of a devil face, topped with silver-gray hair, appeared over my shoulder. A black-gloved hand cupped my chin and pulled my head back, as I felt another gloved hand cupping my buttocks and then helping to guide the cap of a hard cock at the rim of my hole. A long cock slid and slid and slid up into me. I felt the sliver studs of the chest harness rubbing on my back. I cried out my welcome—"Yes, yes, YES!"—and began moving my hips against the building plowing of the cock inside me, pulling at my bindings, wanting some form of control and way to signal that I didn't need to be held captive to want this. A freeing that no form of begging was granting me.

"Excuse me. Exactly what sort of commercials are these?" I asked as I once more became aware of the film producer sitting across from me, leaning into me, smiling his mature Paul Newman smile, and, now, with a gloved hand on my thigh under the table, squeezing my thigh gently—in a rhythm that was reminiscent of the rhythm of the stroking in my St. Andrew's cross fantasy.

"Not commercials, exactly. Commercial films. Ones that make very good money and that could give you exposure for larger roles in larger films."

"I'm not sure I—"

I was getting the drift of this. Exposure. Exposure indeed. But I couldn't form words to respond before he broke in, pressing the sell. I didn't even know what I wanted to say. The feel of that gloved hand on my thigh was robbing my brain of thought.

"It was Jake Plaugher who put us on to your agent. Jake Plaugher is a friend of ours. He's made some films with his. I believe he is a special friend of yours too. Is that not so?"

Jake Plaugher. I tensed. He was saying that he knew what I let Jake Plaugher do to me. It wasn't just that this man wanted me to go with him to audition on my back for a film gig.

His voice was low, almost singsong in texture, drawing me in. "In and out, in and out—the slide of the cock—coupled with the helpless pull at the bindings. That's such a visual image, isn't it? Just like these gloves are. You haven't asked about the gloves. I wear them to provide a visual image of what might be, what is to come, what can be yours if you give yourself to me. And I'm a visual man." Holland's mature Paul Newman smile was mesmerizing, but something in the smile was changing. "And the image of giving over all control to another . . . to a real expert in the sensual . . . a man who can give you what you need . . ."

He didn't finish that sentence. I had interjected a strangled moan, surfaced not only from the images he had spun but also from the black-gloved hand he had moved to my basket. I only then was aware that I had slid down on my chair, my tailbone at the front edge, to permit the hand, which had been slowly working its way up my thigh, to reach my crotch. I had raised one of my feet to his chair, resting it beside his rump, and he was gripping my ankle in his other gloved hand, holding it there, tightly, in thrall, for a brief moment. No matter how brief the moment, though, I felt the sense of the imprisonment, of the control he was asserting.

"Come," Holland said, rising and putting out his gloved hand. "The studio isn't far from here. We can have you back on a plane to New York this evening. We've arranged for Jake Plaugher to meet you at JFK upon your return and to put you up for the night. I understand Jake has unusual ways to put you up. We can be just as inventive as Jake is, though—in fact, you might decide you are too exhausted to accept Jake's offer. But it will be an exhaustion that leaves you humming. And, who knows, maybe you won't want to return to New York at all."

Hearing his raspy laugh—a shudderingly familiar laugh—at his own joke, I looked up into his face. Was this the face of the man I had sat down at the table with?

"Come be a part of our Halloween special. Come. I can fulfill your darkest fantasies—and immortalize them on film. You do have dark fantasies, don't you?"

He knew. I could almost believe now that he had invoked them.

Seeing him now, the expression on his face, the change that had come into it, I wondered. The man in my fantasies. Was he wearing a mask at all in those fantasies—or was this the face of that man?

Trembling, I rose, and put my hand—and the next several hours of my time and freedom; only that, if I was lucky—in his black-leather gloved hand as he turned me with the other hand on my waist and guided me out of the café and into the backseat of a black chauffeured limousine.

Imagine

"Imagine what we could be doing if we moved up to Washington. Think of the commissions up there, Hal."

Hal turned from the window and looked over to his younger, half brother, Jimmy, as he sat at his workbench in the studio, glazing a frame to go perfectly with the landscape acrylic Hal had completed not more than two hours earlier.

A lump rose in Hal's throat. He'd been gazing out of the window, down toward the tenant cottage along the river bank because he couldn't bear to look at Jimmy in the late afternoon light beaming down from the skylight onto his unruly, curly blond head, giving him a halo by bounding off the dust particles floating in the air and bringing out flecks of gold in the young man's hair. Jimmy was an angel. And he made Hal feel like something else altogether.

He was Hal's half brother, dammit. Hal couldn't be having these thoughts. One of them perhaps should be moving to the larger art scene up in Washington, D.C. But only one of them, or Hal didn't know what might happen. He didn't know how much longer he could go on with just the two of them in the house, working symbiotically in the same studio, Hal painting the landscapes and Jimmy preparing the perfect matting and frame to go with them. Hal had sold very little before Jimmy decided that college wasn't for him and moved in and began framing Hal's work. The custom frames had made all of the difference in sales— and in the attention Hal was receiving from art critics and gallery owners. Hal had to admit that Jimmy was right that they might be ready for a big city now—but Hal could not trust himself with Jimmy very much longer. Certainly not in the proximity required for them to work together.

"Perhaps. It's something to think about," Hal answered, trying not reveal that he was speaking with great difficulty, through heavy breathing, and not turning full face toward the younger man, not wanting to reveal the effect Jimmy, in that light, had on his body.

Hal switched his gaze back toward the tenant shack and then, because he heard the cough and roar of a power mower, across the road toward Hampton Grove, the B&B. Hal's own house, the central core of which was built in the eighteenth century by the owner of the mill now in ruins down at the edge of the river, was one of a pocket of antebellum houses on the two streets remaining of a town that had almost been wiped off the map by hand-to-hand fighting in a Civil War battle and that now was preserved for posterity and the tourist trade. The young college guy who did the Grove's yard work during the summer had started up with the mower.

The youth was a long and lanky redhead, with freckles covering a well-worked chest, bare now. To fight the heat, the yard boy had stripped down to skimpy gray cotton athletic shorts. Hal, already thinking arousing thoughts because of the nearness of Jimmy, found his eyes riveted on the youth, to his chest and washboard abs and down to his crotch, and a hand furtively moving to his own basket.

"Can you come over here and see if you like this frame coloring with your landscape?" Jimmy called over to Hal.

"Just a minute. I'm thirsty. I'll go get something from the fridge and be with you in a minute."

Hal wasn't that thirsty, but he had to cool off somehow before going anywhere near his half brother. He moved quickly to the door to the breezeway connecting the older section of the house to the studio, which had been converted from a double garage, and then on into the kitchen, where he threw cubes of ice in a glass and filled it with water. He then applied it to the back of his neck, working to bring his breathing and hardness under control.

He raised his head and looked through the window over the kitchen sink.

It took him a few minutes to notice that he couldn't hear the mower from across the street anymore, and he looked closer at Hampton Grove. The mower was still there, but the yard boy wasn't pushing it. It stood there near the street, in mid swath, across the road.

Hal moved through the dining room and into the study at the back of the house, to a window overlooking the river, where he turned his eyes toward the tenant shack. The tenant's muscular jet-black truck was there now, parked outside the house.

Hal's imagination went into high gear, putting the signs together. Hal knew what his tenant was. He was a construction worker over in Harrisonburg. A large, burly man, hard muscle on muscle—large in the sense of a powerful physique, not in any sense of fat. Dark and hairy and rough looking, with a menacing demeanor and full-coverage tattoos and battle scars.

And Hal knew what the man liked and went after. There were cars and trucks over there at all hours of the day and night whenever the man wasn't working in town. And Hal had seen the men get out of their vehicles and slowly walk up to the door of the shack. And later, he'd seen them stumble out, bowlegged and barely able to walk, but looking oh so satisfied.

The tenant had approached Hal directly, not saying it, but making the offer, letting Hal know he was transparent, that there wasn't an iota of difference between the two of them in what they liked and what they wanted. But Hal had backed away. Afraid. Something about the man scared him. The devil incarnate. Hal lusted after his younger brother, true. But it wasn't the same at all. Hal wanted to take Jimmy, and Hal knew that wasn't how it would proceed if he went with the tenant. Hal knew that going with the tenant would be opening up another door altogether. That man was a dominator and would bottom for no other man. In that way there wasn't any difference between the two of them. And Hal was afraid of the man, afraid that if he gave into him, there would be no turning back.

Thoughts of the long, lanky redheaded yard boy and the dark, menacing tenant flamed in Hal's mind, and he found himself leaving the house and floating across the expanse of grass toward the copse of trees nestling the tenant shack by the ruins of the mill trace at the edge of the river.

He could hear them long before he reached the scrubby flower bed beneath the window that was his goal. Loud cries, approaching screaming, the intent of which Hal could not determine. Pain, yes certainly pain, and fear, at least a touch of that too. But also something else, something more, something dominating. Insistence, and pleasure, and wanting. A want scratched; a dream fulfilled. A total taking and a total giving.

Hal reached the window, which was dusty and streaked with grime. But the light was on in the room, and the view was clear enough. The yard boy reclined in a sling suspended from the ceiling, his arms and legs rising up the four chains at the corners and secured by black strappings. The redhead's skull was flopping down from the sling at the near side, his eyes wild, staring at Hal, and his mouth stretched open in a perpetual scream. The hairy beast of a man standing crouched over the freckled torso of the yard boy at the other end of the sling, moving fast and hard in a staccato rhythm that sent the sling swaying toward Hal with each thrust, each attack met with a pain-pleasure cry from the mouth of the yard boy and each backward retreat answered with a gurgling groan.

Tight muscles gleaming and undulating, tattoos dancing. A thick, long-fingered hand wrapped around the engorged cock of the youth, beating it at a determined, relentless pace. The other hand digging into the quarry's nipples and slapping at the yard boy's bare buttocks and hard-muscled chest. The slap, slap of the hand. The slapslapslap of the fucking cock. Tan-dark, tattoo-laced muscle exploding into freckled and creamy yielding young flesh. The impassioned screams and long moans of the youth. Begging for mercy. Answered with a throaty laugh and a double-time rhythm. Crying out for deeper penetration, fuller possessing. Gasping and groaning when pleas were answered—and surpassed.

The beast looked up from his prey straight at the window. Surely he could see Hal standing there, on the other side of the murky glass. The upturning of the tenant's full-lipped mouth showing recognition. And pleasure. And taunting.

Hal knew he should withdraw; the danger and the enticement were thick in the hot, heavy, humid air near the edge of the river. But he was riveted to the spot, his mouth dry and slack, a hand forcing itself below the waistband of his shorts and encasing and squeezing his cock.

His imagination was making the tenant into more of a monster than he was. It surely was running away with itself, as he viewed the nub of horns at the tenant's temples and the pointedness of his ears—and of his teeth as he opened his maw and smiled cruelly across the writhing body of the yard boy, reaching out beyond the room. To Hal.

Hal no longer saw the redheaded yard boy or even the hairy monster tenant. What he saw now was the golden curly head of Jimmy on the body bound in the sling and he, himself, holding Jimmy's legs up and out with his hands and deviling his own brother's channel with his thrusting cock.

The yard boy's body was lurching, and he was gasping and groaning and crying out of his impending coming, and the tenant beast kept pumping. Pumping with his hand and pumping with his cock. The youth cried out, and globular white cum shoot out between the long, thick, pumping fingers of the tenant and fell like molten snow across the youth's heaving chest. The monster's cock pumped on, his hands cupping the slim hips of the youth and raising and pulling the yard boy's pelvis back hard onto his thrusting cock with each brutal stroke.

The youth went limp, no longer writhing, no longer even there, his head flopped back with each thrust, his face turned toward Hal, but his eyes unseeing, only the whites showing now.

The monster tenant bellowed his own impending release and reared back. Hal glimpsed a gigantic, rosy-red bulb as it jerked and spouted one, two, three, fountains of snow-white cum in an arc across the youth's chest, reaching out for Hal, goblets of thick, white cum splattering against the window panes with an audible thump.

Then the hairy beast was moving around the sling and toward the window, gliding on what Hal's mind visioned were cloven hooves. The long, thick fingers of one of his hands holding the largest, thickest cock Hal had ever seen, lovingly, accusingly erect. Hairy black balls—shockingly four of them—each as big as tennis balls swung as he strutted, slapping against his gigantic, muscle-bound, tattooed hams.

Hal watched, his mouth opening in an unvoiced scream, as the window glass began to dissolve before his eyes.

With the last vestige of control, he pulled his eyes away from the tenant and turned and soared back to the house—not to the studio, which held its own dangers and forbidden temptation, but up the stairs to his bedroom and the bath beyond. He threw himself into his shower stall; turned the water on full blast, pulling the face and naked, writhing body of his half brother into his mind; masturbated himself to a groaning ejaculation; and collapsed into the corner of the stall.

* * * *

Early in the morning, Hal struggled out of bed, weary and unsatisfied in sleep. He felt hung over, the aroma of coffee set on automatic perk the night before, and the urge of going to the door of Jimmy's bedroom fighting for control. He was groggy, only half aware of what he was doing in the murky light of the hour past dawn. Cold in his nakedness now that he wasn't under the sheet, he reached for his silken bathrobe and draped it over his shoulders.

He was on the threshold of Jimmy's door, looking at Jimmy, naked and tangled in the sheets. White sheets, marbled body. Golden, tussled curls and just the dew of light hair on his limbs and tufting on the V down to his delicate, boy's cock. Hal began by wondering how large it could grow, what his channel smelled like. Whether he would moan in pleasure as Hal filled that channel. He could almost feel his hand on Jimmy's knee, moving slowly up his thigh over the downy blond hair. Jimmy's eyes on his, his lips opening as Hal bent over him, letting the edges of his open silken robe brush along his brother's sides. Seeing Jimmy's cock fill out and his hands reach down and encircle both cocks

34

together as Hal's lips met Jimmy's. Jimmy trembling and his back arching as Hal's tongue slipped between his opening lips and his cock slid into his opening channel. Jimmy's legs hooking around Hal's waist and above his buttocks. A shared gasp as . . .

Hal stubbed his toe as it dragged across the threshold of the door, enticing his body to follow it into the room. More awake now, Hal groaned at the frustration of what he was struggling against. And he turned and stumbled down the stairs and into the kitchen, where the automatically perked coffee awaited him, inviting him back into the world of sanity and controlled imagination.

Hal poured a cup and pattered out into the breezeway. Peering out into the haze of the misty morning, his eye was caught by the yellow of the Corvette parked outside the tenant's shack, next to the tenant's black truck. There was only one person who drove a yellow Corvette around here—the young lawyer from the end house on the other street of the small hamlet. A perky wife and three small children.

Hal fought the urge to walk out onto the grass and toward the tenant shack. With difficulty he forced his feet to turn toward the studio. The light was on inside the studio. It should not have been. And when Hal entered the room, he stood there, gawking in horror.

There were three of them. Just sketches. Charcoal on art paper, clipped to three standing easels. Despite being sketches, they were finely detailed and expertly done, with strong, assured strokes. His work no doubt, but when had he done these? Jimmy couldn't see these. No one could see these.

One was of Jimmy, in nearly the same pose he was in even now upstairs in his bedroom. The other two were unmistakably of both of them. The two half brothers, draped together in the silken robe around Hal's shoulders, open, enveloping the nakedness of both of them. With Hal fucking Jimmy—and Jimmy, angelic Jimmy, loving it.

Hal moved quickly, tearing the sheets of paper from the easels, starting to ball them up, but discovering he could not do it. He smoothed the sheets out and stumbled back into the breezeway.

He felt that he was going completely out of control. He now knew why he had risen so tired. He'd been up most of the night trying to exorcise his demons. He could clearly remember now. But he'd risen and come all the way down to the studio without remembering.

What if Jimmy had been the first to rise? How much longer could Hal hold himself off? This couldn't continue.

Reaching the breezeway, Hal looked out of the glass wall toward the tenant's house once more. They were both outside. The young golden-curled lawyer belly down on the hood of his Corvette, and the tenant standing between his legs, fucking him hard. As Hal watched, the tenant shrugged a silken robe off his shoulders and let it slip down to cascade around his feet, revealing that he was bulbous butted and hairy-pelted from the hips down, his legs goatlike, standing on cloven feet. Hal could hear the moans from where he stood. Each drawn-out moan matched with the contraction of the tenant's buttocks muscles, straining under the forward thrust, the moan filtering off into a sigh as the butt cheeks relaxed and filled out again, readying for the next contraction/thrust.

Could Jimmy hear the moans? Something had to be done, something soon, something fast. This could not go on. Hal looked down at his erect cock—and beyond to hairy-pelted legs and cloven feet. And he heard the coffee cup hit the clay-tiled floor of the breezeway and shatter. He looked down again. What had he imagined? No pelt or cloven feet. And looking out toward the tenant's shack. No tenant or young, golden-curled lawyer—or even yellow Corvette. They had vanished.

Hal fled up the stairs, as quietly as he could, and entered his bedroom. Looking for somewhere to stash his drawings from the previous night. Jimmy could not see them. Neither, though, could Hal part with them now. Drawings hidden, he shrugged off the silken robe on the carpeted floor next to his bed and lay on his back, Jimmy's face and body floating before his eyes, as he slowly masturbated himself to a sighing ejaculation.

* * * *

Working from photographs of the fields of the valley set against the backdrop of the Blue Ridge Mountains, Hal willfully was deep into painting, moving quickly now with his brush to finish with this color before the dappled light filtering through the overarching oaks and through the skylight of the studio had waned.

The house was quiet. Jimmy had gone into Staunton. He had been in a jubilant mood, telling Hal before he left that he hoped he'd have some important news when he returned home. Hal had only half heard him. Hal had taken to drink—drink to dull his senses and combat his imagination, as he could no longer look at Jimmy and not see him naked—the golden orb of Jimmy's head at Hal's pelvis as Jimmy took his cock in his throat. The marble skin of Jimmy's thighs as they parted for Hal and his thrusting cock.

Jimmy, Hal's half brother. Hal had to keep muttering "He's my brother; this isn't right" to himself, almost as a mantra as he remained half drunk, half buried in his work.

He was mercifully alone now, in the silence, deftly stroking at the canvas with the purple underlay of the coloring he was building up at the base of the Blue Ridge, between field and mountain.

But it wasn't really silence. Hal was listening for the sound for several minutes before he identified it as moaning. The moan of sex.

He put his paint brush down on the ledge below the canvas on the easel and he was right there, at the window of the tenant shack, one hand on his cock, the other at the nipple of his bare chest, watching. Surprisingly not in shock, knowing what he'd see as soon as he became cognizant of the moaning.

Jimmy was naked, his marbled beauty stretched out, the toes of his feet barely reaching the dusty wooden floor, suspended from the ceiling by chains and bindings around his wrists.

The tenant was crouched in front of him, blocking the view of Jimmy's midsection from Hal. Sucking sounds of the hairy tenant's mouth on Jimmy's cock and the moans of pleasure from Jimmy melding in an arousing melody.

Jimmy shuddered his ejaculation, and the tenant stood and moved around him. Hal's eyes went to Jimmy's cock, seeing that it did fill out quite respectably. But Hal's gasp was dedicated to the view of the tenant's cock, thick as Jimmy's wrist.

Deep moaning filling the air, with Hal realizing with a start that much of the moaning was his own. Wanting to do something. Wanting to warn Jimmy. Knowing that Jimmy couldn't take a cock like that, that it would tear him asunder. His little brother. Jimmy, his half brother. The brother that Hal himself wanted to fuck.

The tenant was crouched behind Jimmy now, his long, heavy-fingered hands grasping Jimmy's legs above the back of the knees and lifting his legs up and out. The monster's mouth going to Jimmy's hole, and Jimmy groaning and writhing under the attentions there.

Rising, the tenant's face sharpened into a leering malevolence, and once again Hal had the sensation that nubs of horns rose from his temples and the hair of his legs that weren't human legs thickened and dropped down into feet that weren't human feet. He was lifting Jimmy higher and spreading his legs wider, and the club of a gigantic cock was at Jimmy's hole. The long, thick fingers were encasing Jimmy's butt cheeks and spreading them wide, revealing the rosebud of his gate. The bulb the tenant presented at the hole was monstrously huge. But it was slowly sucking itself into Jimmy's hole, which was blossoming out, opening to the invasion, as Jimmy's body heaved and shuddered and his rosebud opened up. The impossible began to become possible as more and more of that killing tool moved up into Jimmy, who screamed and writhed and burbled his pain-pleasure, moving ever so slowly to pleasure-pain as more and more of the thick pole moved up into him.

Fully sheathed, Jimmy's body took on a shimmering luster, and he laid his golden-curled head back into the cleft of the tenant's shoulder, opened his eyes to Hal, and let him know in no certain terms that it was Hal who was taking him. The monster began to pump slowly and then ever quicker. Hal felt one with the movement, his gasps and groans meeting the rhythm and tenor of the fucking machine. He didn't realize just how much he was melding into the scene, though, until he looked up and watched the monster's face slowly morph into his own features.

"How can you paint in this gloom?"

Hal lifted his head, groggy from so much he was leaving unsaid, undone.

"No, I'm done for now. I was just sitting here . . . thinking . . . or something."

Hal looked up at Jimmy, who was nearly dancing around the room, overflowing with exuberance, and beauty . . . aching beauty. Hal stood and moved to the window and looked out toward the river, in too much pain to look at Jimmy.

"Guess what," Jimmy bubbled. "I've been to Staunton. Seen Gretchen. You remember Gretchen, don't 'ya? We were at school together?"

"Oh, yes, Gretchen. The Gretchen of your first-semester college crush, would that be?"

"Yeah, that Gretchen. Well, guess what. She's got an art teaching job at a high school down in Winston Salem. And . . . and she wants me to go down with her. I don't know. What we're doing here . . ."

"I think that's a great idea," Hal said, and he turned and gave the best smile he could muster to his little half brother. And then his smile broadened. Because he realized that this was lifting a burden off his shoulders. He should be miserable, he knew, but that's not what he felt. This was best for all. His urge would recede, he knew it. It didn't have to be Jimmy. It couldn't be Jimmy. It was tearing him apart that it might be Jimmy.

"Oh, that's great then. I didn't know . . ."

Hall looked hard at Jimmy. Jimmy really did think it was great, he could see. There was nothing in Jimmy's mind that had been in his. This was best. Yes, the very best thing that could happen. He turned his face back to the window.

"What are you looking at so intently?" Jimmy asked, coming over to stand close beside his older brother.

Hal's spirits soared. Jimmy was standing right next to him. For weeks Hal had trembled and fought his urges just to have Jimmy in the same room with him. The cloud was lifted. Now he was sure of it.

"I'm just looking at that shack of mine over by the river edge."

"Thinking of fixing it up? Putting a tenant in it or something?" Jimmy asked. "I think you did say something about doing that."

"No. I think it's beyond repair. See, the roof has caved in over that bedroom area already. Hasn't been anyone living in there for decades. No, I think the best thing to do is just to have it torn down and the trash hauled off. All it's good for now is to get someone hurt. And we wouldn't want that, would we?"

"I thought you once said that, with a little imagination, it could be quite a desirable place," Jimmy said.

"I said that?" Hal answered. "I don't know what I was thinking if I said imagination could bring any good out of that pile of festering wood. No. No. I think it comes down and disappears."

Devilish Grin

"Would you look at that?"

"Look at what?" Lucian asked, leaning over close to Dan at the table underneath the umbrella on the golf and tennis club's café terrace. He thought that if he could get cheek to cheek with the hunk, it would be a start on making him.

"That Zack Wilson over there. He's strutting around like he owns the place."

"Perhaps that's because he does own a big chunk of it. Or haven't you heard?"

"No," Dan said, his voice full of the morose. "I hadn't heard. Where did he get the money to buy into the club? How can he be zipping ahead financially when the rest of us are barely hanging on by our fingernails in this recession?"

Envy, Lucian thought. Why didn't he guess that would be the key to Dan? It looked increasingly like he was going to get lucky. Envy. Envy and bitterness and the feeling of failure. Not to mention, of course, the need for money to support living above one's means—which led to all the rest. Those were also strong tools in his business.

"So, you know of the straits he was in a year ago, do you?"

"Sure," Dan answered, swinging around from the baleful look he'd been giving Zack, who was flirting with two forty-something, but still quite presentable, women at a table over by the steps down to the eighteenth hole. They twittered back at him like he was some sort of celebrity or something. Like he was the most delicious thing on the menu. Dan snorted derisively before he continued. "Yes, a year ago he was trying to get me to take his old Chrysler off his hands so he could make the month's rent. Now he drives a Porsche and lives in a house twice the size of the one he couldn't afford then."

"And yet a year ago he was sitting with me on this terrace in exactly the same circumstances as you are today." Lucian nudged his chair around a bit closer to Dan's—on the terrace wall side, where no one from the restaurant would see what his hands would be doing under the table top in case this conversation got that far.

"The same circumstance? You mean that he was asking your company for a loan?"

"Yes."

"And you gave him one despite the financial condition he was in?"

"Yes. We invest in people and their potential, Dan. Zack had great potential. And I could see that in him. I think you could have it in you too, Dan." Potential indeed, Lucian was thinking. Dan was one nice piece of ass.

"And from there Zack was able to accomplish this miraculous turnaround?"

"Well, it was more complex than that, Dan. Zack needed more help than just money." Lucian lowered his voice to a whisper so that Dan had to lean in toward him to hear what he had to say.

"What do you mean? Do you mean your company helped him in more ways than just a financial loan?"

"Yes, of course. We are a well-connected firm, Dan. We have ways of helping our clients expand their money exponentially. We like to get a very good return on our investment, and we take a very personal interest in our loan clients. Zack had what it takes, of course, but we were—I was— pleased to help him along." Lucian was barely whispering now, and he made sure his face was at an angle from Dan. Dan had to scoot his chair around toward Lucian, just as Lucian had planned.

"And this is how Zack recovered so fully and expanded his investment capital—by working closely with your firm?"

"As I said, he did come with assets. Zack is a very attractive and compelling man. And it has largely been because he was working closely—very closely—with me, Dan."

"How is this possible? How can your firm help someone make such a turnaround so quickly in an economy like the one we're suffering? Is this some sort of voodoo magic?"

"Don't joke about such things," Lucian said. His tone was sharp, and he gave Dan a glowering look, trying to appear foreboding. His swarthy complexion and jet black hair, including a pointed goatee, and his piercingly cold blue eyes helped him in this regard. "Do you reject the possibility of the occult, Dan—that there are forces at work that are beyond the understanding and control of mere man?"

"I . . . I . . .I don't know. All of that is . . ." Dan felt himself beginning to sweat. He backed right down. The last thing he wanted to do today was alienate Lucian Abaddon. He'd been all over the state before contacting Lucian. And nothing. There had been no help for him. He was keeping up appearances. But he was almost as close to reneging on the house payment the month after next as Zack had been when he'd come crawling to him to buy his Chrysler. There were rumors about Lucian and his company—although Dan's best research hadn't dug out anything on the company beyond Lucian himself. There was talk of how Lucian was a miracle man, but there were also whispers of the demands he made. Of something unusual.

Dan knew Lucian was gay—and that he had some very strange ideas. He had tried everything else he could think of before calling Lucian. But no one else in the state had given him the time of day on helping him dig himself out of his financial hole. If there was a question of what Dan would do at today's meeting—just how much of his soul he would sell to land a loan—it had all been wrestled with and fundamentally answered before he had gotten to this point.

"Hokum, Dan? Are you really so sure? Look at Zack, Dan. You know how he was a year ago, and you can see how he is today. Do you think that transition was natural? I told you that my firm was well connected. Perhaps you don't know just how well connected. Look at Zack, Dan. You are a good analyst. You have been doing some checking, haven't you? I know you have. You'd be surprised what I know about you. What have you learned about how my help has worked out for others?"

"You do have a good success record, Lucian. That was quite evident. I just don't . . ."

"And your research has given you a good idea of what signing with me entails, doesn't it? Be honest about that, Dan."

Dan didn't answer. He couldn't maintain eye contact with Lucian. He just lowered his face, looking down at the table top, realizing only now that the fingers of one of Lucian's hands were laying lightly on top of one of his hands.

"Look at Zack, Dan. What comes to mind when you look at Zack over there and compare what his situation was a year ago and how things are working for him now? What would be your first thought."

"My first thought?" Dan asked. "That he'd sold his soul, I guess." The words almost caught in Dan's throat. He immediately wanted to pull those words back, but something about the situation and Zack's success had just forced this out of him—what he'd been thinking even before he showed up to this meeting, the suggestiveness and all, what Lucian was saying to him, Lucian's look—the whole satanic edge to him. Dan laughed, trying to cover his nervousness, but revealing it in the shakiness—almost hysteria—of the laugh rather than hiding it.

"That's not funny," Lucian said, covering his face with his most serious mask. "It's something to consider, of course. But it isn't something to joke about it. I can tell you that Zack doesn't joke about it."

Dan sat there, paralyzed. It was only now that he realized that Lucian's hand had moved to rest on his knee under the table.

"Look at Zack again," Lucian said.

Dan lifted his head, as directed, and stared at Zack, still chatting up the two giggling women.

Good, Lucian thought. He's still with me and following my directions.

"Does it look like Zack is putting the make on those women, Dan?"

"Yes."

"And does it look like he could have either one of them, if he wanted them?"

"Yes." This was said with a bit of a yelp, because Lucian's hand was higher on his thigh now.

"And do you think he will fuck either one or both of them?"

"Yes. Probably."

"Maybe, Dan. But maybe not. Do you think he has enjoyed being with women all that much for the past year—considering all of the options? And let's say, just for the sake of argument, that he has explored other options. Does it look like he has suffered from that?"

Dan didn't answer. All of his senses were on that hot hand on his thigh.

"Do you want a loan, Dan? Do you want my help in expanding your capital?"

"Yes."

"We haven't discussed collateral. Do you want to do that now?"

"No . . . yes . . . Um, I don't know what to say."

"Do I really need to discuss collateral with you? Do you really not know what collateral Zack put up—when last year at this time he had nothing, that his only asset was himself, his own body?"

Dan didn't answer. He just sat there, breathing heavily. There was no need for him to answer verbally. His body was answering for him. Lucian had a hand spread on his basket, under the table. and was taking the measure of Dan through the thin material of his golfing trousers.

"If you want the loan and my help, it's your soul I want as collateral, Dan. I think that should be quite clear between us. If you want this, we will have to move our discussions to my bedroom. How about it? It's decision time. What do you say?"

"Shall I put these drinks on my tab?" Dan answered weakly.

Dan was shy and wooden from the start when they reached Lucian's house. Dan wasn't the least surprised at the gothic décor of the house or the four-poster bed with its heavy brocade drapes, but the whole aspect of the house intimidated him. The decor only added to his foreboding about just how deeply he was getting into something beyond his understanding and control.

What really surprised him, though, was that, once Lucian was stripped down, there seemed nothing special or satanic about him. His arms and chest were covered with curly black hair, but there were no pelted goat legs or hooves or horns. It was almost a letdown. If Dan was going to sell his soul, he would have appreciated some of the trappings that went with it—some sort of sign that it was all true. Idiotic, he knew, but there it was. These were the thoughts going through his mind as he tip-toed along the tightrope of hysteria.

Lucian didn't give him long to contemplate the selling of his soul, though. He sat on the edge of the bed once they were both naked; pushed Dan to his knees in front of him, between his legs; and fed his cock into Dan's mouth. Dan gagged and showed reluctance, but Lucian directed him well and led him through the process with encouraging words and rewarding sounds of pleasure.

Dan was even more reluctant when, fully prepared himself, Lucian pulled him up, laid him on his back on the bed, and, stretching out beside him, moved his hand to Dan's crotch and his lips to the hollow of Dan's neck and then up to his mouth. Dan went rigid and Lucian sweet-talked him, with Dan relaxing and increasingly emitting involuntary moans as Lucian's hand did its magic on Dan's cock. Soon Dan was writhing and groaning and his hips were rolling in rhythm with the pumping of Lucian's hand, and, giving a little cry, he arched his back and shot his load across his quivering belly.

"You OK?" Lucian murmured.

"Yes," Dan answered somewhat uncertainly.

"That's done now, isn't it?"

"Yes," Dan answered, and then, in surprise, he uttered an explicative and Lucian covered his mouth with the palm of his hand as he rolled over on top of Dan and spread his legs with the other hand.

"What . . . what . . . ?" Dan exclaimed when Lucian removed his hand to open the condom packet.

"It's not done. Not yet. Not by a long shot. Do you want the loan or not, Dan?" Lucian asked, his voice suddenly dominating, hard edged.

"Yes," whimpered Dan, "But . . ."

"Zack has a Porsche, Dan. What was it you said you coveted? A Corvette? Think of the Corvette, Dan."

Dan was reduced to light pants, and then he cried out and went rigid and had to be cajoled to relax as Lucian entered him and began to open him up for a prolonged session of slow fucking in multiple positions.

Later, as they lay side by side and Dan fought to return his breathing to a regular rhythm and tried to forget both the pain in his ass and the fact that he had come to enjoy it—and wanted to do it again—Lucian spoke.

"Collateral, Dan. Every Tuesday afternoon for the term of the loan—if that's what I want. problem with that?"

"No, not really. It was better than expected. But . . ."

"But what, Dan?"

"But, oh, I don't know. Selling my soul and all. I guess I expected something—fireworks, clashing of symbols, billowing smoke and fire or something."

"You don't really believe in all of that occult shit, do you, Dan?" Lucian said. He leaned over and kissed Dan on a nipple and then raised his head and looked into Dan's face—and laughed.

"Oh, god," Dan muttered.

"Nothing satanic about the arrangement," Lucian said. "But God doesn't have a damn thing to do with it either. It's just a business deal and a weekly fuck rather than having to put up any other collateral."

"And no Corvette, either, I take it," Dan answered. He was beginning to see the humor in the situation—and how incredibly naïve he'd been in his frustrated need. If he hadn't been very pleasantly surprised with how well a man can make love to another, he might have been angry. But Lucian had fucked all of the anger and fear out of him. And, although he certainly wouldn't reveal it to Lucian, Dan was already looking forward to next Tuesday afternoon's tryst.

"You can buy anything you think you can afford, Dan. I'd be careful with the money I give you, though. The stock market can be so iffy—especially in these times."

"And Zack?"

"Rich uncle died is the way I heard it," Lucian answered. "It didn't have anything to do with a loan."

"Shit."

The Devil Made Me Do It

"Oh yes, oh god yes." Aaron was panting hard under the touch of Jack's hand on his cock. His frat roommate, the guy who had brought him into the fraternity and who had volunteered to room with him his initiative semester here, was driving him wild.

It was late in the night; they both had been studying, or at least Aaron had been. He was cramming for a big chemistry exam he had the next morning. But Aaron was having a hard time concentrating. The room was small. There was room for just one desk separating two twin beds. They had to call dibs on the desk, with the other one forced downstairs to the common rooms to study, where they were more likely to get involved in a wrestling match or chugging contest than working the books.

Jack, as a full brother in the fraternity, had dibs whenever he wanted on the desk. But Aaron was lucky in that Jack was more the jock than the scholar and didn't fight Aaron for position there very often. With the exam tomorrow, Aaron had won the desk. But he was losing the battle for concentration.

The night was hot, and the frat house, which could best be described as utilitarian even under the piles of rubbish and notwithstanding the damaged floors, walls, and ceilings that came with college men living in rented quarters, wasn't air conditioned. So the lone window over the desk was open and Aaron was down to athletic shorts, while Jack was stripped down even further, to his briefs.

Jack was stretched out on the bed, reading a gay male glossy magazine and languidly scratching at his hard belly and fingering himself through the flimsy white cotton of the briefs. His occasional grunts and groans cut through the silence of the room.

This was why Aaron couldn't concentrate on his studies. Jack had fucked him before—but just the once, and it was the only time Aaron had let a guy do that to him. It had been the arrogant primitive animal in Jack that had attracted Aaron. Aaron had gotten—and even given—head a few times before that, and he knew he was interested in what a man could do with another man, but it wasn't until he'd been a junior camp counselor the previous summer and met up with Jack as a senior camp counselor and discovered that they would be attending the same college that Aaron began to fall under the spell of another male enough to allow a hard cock up his channel.

Jack was all of the things Aaron thought he wanted to be that summer at the camp—and Jack showed an interest in him and helped him surmount all of the hurdles in learning to handle at-risk city boys let loose in the woods. Aaron had happened on Jack fucking one of the other counselors in the shower stalls near the close of the summer, and Aaron spent the last two weeks of camp dreaming of what it would be like to be with Jack and sloughing off any resistance he might have had to such an encounter.

In the end Aaron was a pushover. All Jack had to do was to walk into Aaron's cabin after most of the boys and all of the counselors Aaron had been bunking with had departed the camp, open his fly, drag out his cock, and tell Aaron he wanted him to suck him off, and Aaron was doing his bidding. Aaron hadn't really envisioned it going further than that, but by the time Jack finished feeling him up and working his cock up with his hand, Aaron was virtually begging to be fucked. And Jack had obliged.

Jack was built big, but he had been as gentle he could have been when it had come to the point of entry, and there had been far more pleasure and arousal and jacking off for Aaron in the experience than he'd imagined would be the case the first time he did it.

Not that there had been any question in Aaron's mind that he'd do it. He had been curious about it for some time. There in the rustic woods, completely imprisoned in Jack's arms, and being pumped slowly to the rhythm of the croaking of frogs at the nearby pond and the pressure of a hand working him up and making him come was as good a way for him to lose his virginity as any. And Aaron was up for a frequent repeating of the act with Jack.

But the next day Jack had decamped, and since they'd gotten to college Jack hadn't touched Aaron. He'd teased him and he'd encouraged Aaron to pledge this fraternity, and he'd volunteered to be his big brother and his roommate. But it was late October already and other than a few pats and fondles and a shared hand job their first night in the room, it was almost as if they'd never had sex before.

Or it was almost as if Jack was building up to something big.

Aaron felt himself breathing heavily and taking sidelong looks at Jack on the bed as Jack slowly paged through the magazine and ran his hand over his nicely muscled body. Using every ounce of his will, Aaron buried his eyes in his chem book.

"Com'her."

Aaron looked up, startled. He hadn't sensed Jack raise himself to a sitting position on the bed, very close to Aaron. Everything in their room was very close to everything else, almost oppressively so, which added to the aroused heaviness Aaron felt.

Aaron's eyes went big. Jack was sitting there, legs spread wide, patting the space between them with one hand and beckoning to Aaron with the other. The bulge of his dick beneath the thin cotton material of the briefs caused Aaron to gasp.

"Come on over here. Give me some sugar, will ya? I'm horny readin' this mag. Want a little of you over here."

Aaron felt himself going hard. With a sigh and a hoarse catch in his breath, he pulled away from his book. All he needed to do was half stand and turn, and Jack had his arms around his waist, pulling him down into a sitting position on the edge of the bed between Jack's spread thighs.

Jack was bigger and stronger than Aaron. When Aaron was sitting between his legs, Jack encircled him with heavily muscled arms and held him close. This was what Aaron remembered most of their earlier encounter—Jack holding him close, not letting him move a muscle, with the only things in motion being Jack's cock and rolling pelvis and Aaron's split and quivering butt cheeks.

"Oh, Jack," Aaron whimpered. He could feel Jack's hard cock at the base of his spine even through Jack's briefs. "Oh, god."

Jack's lips went to the hollow of Aaron's neck, and one of his hands pushed Aaron's shorts and briefs below his knees and went to Aaron's cock, palming the rising member and thrumbing the piss slit with a thumb.

"Oh yes, oh god yes." Aaron was panting hard under the touch of Jack's hand on his cock.

Jack whispered endearments in Aaron's ear—of how nice Aaron's body was and did Aaron remember what Jack had done to that body before and detailing step by step what he was going to do to it now. Aaron moaned his arousal as Jack held him very still and pumped his cock with a hand and made like he was going to invade his piss slit with an index finger.

Aaron writhed within the limited freedom Jack allowed him. Murmuring of how good it was; warning Jack when he was close to coming; trying to move with the rhythm of the pumping of his cock as he came close to ejaculation, although Jack was holding him too firmly; shuddering and crying out as he ejaculated out onto the thin throw rug behind the desk chair.

And then crying out again—this time in shock and indignation—as a coarse-thread bag came over his head and was pulled down to his waist, pinning his arms against his side, and he began to have trouble breathing between his exclamations and expletives. Hands on him—more hands than Jack had. Roughly handling him and lifting him and carrying him, struggling, but without effect, out of the room, down the hall, and out into the night.

* * * *

Aaron was in the trunk of a car, his wrists and ankles bound and a burlap bag over his head. It was crowded in there because he wasn't the only one in the trunk. The other guy was swearing under his breath, and Aaron recognized the voice of the fraternity's other pledge, a black guy named Sam who was rushed because he was the star fullback of the college's football team. Sam was a big bruiser of a guy; not exactly who one would want to share a car truck with. Aaron also thought he was hot, but Sam had shown not a spark of interest in Aaron; all he could talk about were the girls he balled, and Aaron didn't have the slightest doubt that Sam could fuck any girl on campus he wanted to fuck.

"That you, Sam?" Aaron asked.

"Yeah. I thought that would be you too, Aaron. Those fuckers. I could tell by the way they were pussyfooting around that they was plannin' something."

"I guess this is it, then," Aaron whispered.

"I guess so."

"Well, after tonight we should be in."

"Yeah, I guess."

The car moved over a smooth road, but soon it made a right turn and was on gravel, and Aaron and Sam were being bounced around. They heard boisterous talking and raucous laughter from inside the car's passenger compartment. Aaron could identify the voices well enough. His fraternity brothers. This was his pledge semester. He'd expected to be hazed. They were driving Sam and him out into the countryside, and they'd have to find their own way back. Simple enough. He could manage this.

When they stopped and the trunk lid was opened, the burlap bag came off Aaron's head and shoulders and someone was untying his ankles. He slipped when they got him on the ground and Aaron stumbled against Tony, the frat president, Mr. Campus, who thought so much of himself and was so rich. Aaron suspected none of the other guys really liked him, but his father owned the fraternity house and rented it to them at a ridiculously low rate—and didn't seem to mind that they were slowly trashing the place. Tony had his father wound around his finger. Tony could do no wrong that couldn't be overlooked as just a devilish prank.

"Get off me, pledge," Tony growled at Aaron and pushed him into the scrub brush at the edge of a wooded area off the unlit parking lot where they'd parked. Aaron struggled up and looked around him. There were five of the senior brothers, including Jack, who was helping Bert, the fraternity's egghead—the guy who wrote papers for the brothers who couldn't be bothered—pull a struggling Sam out of the car trunk. Two other guys, Pete and Tom, guys who stayed pretty much in the background and played the angles on whoever seemed to be strongest in a fight or argument, were standing back now, too. Tom was carrying a couple of car blankets and Pete was holding a case of beer above one shoulder. Tony obviously was in charge. And Aaron shivered in the cool evening, in only his athletic shorts and briefs, because he knew Tony didn't like him much. Well, he didn't like Tony much either.

"See the path, dotcha?" Tony hissed. "Down that. Now."

So, it was going to be more than just deserting them to walk back to the college, Aaron thought, as he stumbled, Sam just behind him, into the tree line. They came upon a small picnic area with a grassy area next to it, and Tony directed Tom to spread the blankets on the grass and Pete to set the beer on one of the picnic tables and to start doling the cans out.

"Not you, pledge," Tony yelled at Aaron, even though Aaron hadn't made any move to take one.

"You can have one, though, Sam. While you strip."

"I ain't doin' no strippin'," Sam declared.

"You will if you want to be in this fraternity," Tony said, his voice menacing.

Sam mumbled something obscene and then declared he wouldn't be doing anything but stripping. But he began to pull his jeans off his legs, complying with the demand.

It was evident from the outset, though, that they were waltzing around Sam. It wasn't just his size. They really wanted him in the fraternity. He was a star scholarship athlete and every frat had to have one of those. Jack filled the bill now, being captain of the basketball team. But he was a senior. They needed another one when he was gone, and obviously Sam was going to be that for them.

So, Aaron knew that the brunt of this hazing was going to fall on him.

Tony pulled him over onto the blanket while Sam was stripping down and told him to go down on his knees—and then to go down on Bert, who had come around to in front of Aaron and was unzipping himself and pulling his cock out.

"Jack says you do this real well, Aaron. That you love doin' it. We needed a frat punch—to relieve tension and all that—and Jack said you'd do that for us."

Aaron looked around for Jack to give him an accusing stare, but he already had his arms around Pete and was pushing him back toward one of the picnic tables. Aaron's face went red. His folks had paid his frat dues and room and board in advance. He felt humiliated, but he couldn't afford to just walk out on this deal. And he did want to be in the fraternity. It wasn't like he hadn't done this before either.

Thus, when Bert held his cock out, Aaron took it in his mouth and started giving him head.

"Strip off those shorts and down on all fours," Tony commanded. Aaron complied, and Bert went down on his knees as Aaron descended without losing purchase on Bert's hardening cock.

"Now, Sam, we want you to fuck Aaron." Aaron gave a little shudder, but he persevered.

Sam, however, balked. "No, ain't gonna do that," he declared.

"What's the matter?" Tony asked. "Don't you like him?"

"No, he ain't my type."

"What's that supposed to mean."

"He ain't female; ain't got no cunt."

"Well, suit yourself then," Tony said. "But you've got to watch."

Aaron was surprised at himself, but he was actually disappointed that Sam had said no. Out of all of the guys here, Sam was the only one other than Jack who turned him on. He could go with Sam. And Jack wasn't exactly on his good list at the moment. Jack had Pete laying on his back on the picnic table, legs spread, and was already fucking him in long strokes. Aaron felt humiliated that Jack had just done what he'd done with him to set him up for a bitch role in the fraternity.

He had no more time than that to think about it, though, because he cried out and lurched when Tony crouched over his hips from the rear, pushed his cock inside his channel, and began doggy fucking him. After Tony came Bert. And then Tom. He was offered to Sam again, who repeated his refusal.

And Jack showed no interest in taking a turn on Aaron at all.

Aaron was still laying on the ground, dozing in exhaustion and residual pain from the gang banging, the blanket having been jerked out from underneath him when the guys were finished with him. Silence reigned, other than the normal forest sounds, when he became fully conscious. The sound of car doors closing had been what brought him alert. He stumbled up onto his feet and lurched down the path. When he came to the parking lot, the car was across the lot and making a turn on the road—back toward the college, Aaron hoped, because this was the only clue they were giving him on how he was going to get out of here.

He was naked, but he had the presence in mind to go back to the clearing and see that they'd left him his athletic shorts—but not his briefs.

When he came back to the lot, he realized that Sam wasn't there. They'd let him go back with them. And once again, the humiliation poured over Aaron. He was being shown exactly where he fit in the fraternity. He felt trapped and conflicted on whether he wanted to continue pledging—but not knowing what to do if he didn't.

He walked out onto the road, being thankful that they at least had left him in his hiking boots and socks. The parking lot was long and narrow, and Aaron entered it at the end that connected to the gravel road. So, he didn't see the long, sleek black limousine parked in the darkness at the other end of the lot.

* * * *

Aaron had to walk maybe two miles down the gravel road toward what he hoped was an asphalted main road with traffic on it this time of night. Once or twice he thought he heard the gravel crunch behind him, but when he turned, he saw nothing. He did what little he could, under the circumstances. He walked a little faster and a little closer to the side of the road, where he hopefully would have an option of flagging an approaching vehicle down or jumping into the dense forest at the side of the road, depending on whatever split decision he made about the approaching vehicle.

As he walked, he became progressively more ticked with the fraternity brothers. He'd never been manhandled like that before, but after the first dick, the rest seemed like just so much more humiliation. It was less the way he'd been used that set him off and more the difference in treatment between him and Sam— like Sam mattered and he didn't. And then there was Jack's sudden disinterest in him, topped with his going at Pete. Pete was a nebbish, part of the wallpaper in the fraternity house. There because his family owned a beer distribution business. How could Jack prefer Pete to him? But the worst of it, under the circumstances, was Sam's rejection of him.

Well, he'd show them. He'd act like this never happened, and then when he passed out as a pledge, he'd get his dig in at them—every one of them. Nothing they could blame on him, but he'd know he'd done it. Something humiliating for each of them. He'd devil those guys good, he would.

Aaron had reached the main road. There was the decision on which way to go. He had just about decided that there was more light on the horizon above the road to the right than to the left, so that was more likely to be his college town, when he heard the crunching noise on the gravel again. That decided him, and he struck off in that direction. It was just as well, because he wouldn't have to cross the divided road if he went in this direction. And now that he thought about it, he seemed to remember a left turn onto the gravel road when he'd been in the car trunk.

Aaron hadn't walked more than a hundred yards when a big semitrailer truck came bearing down on him. He turned and bravely stuck out his thumb. The truck managed to pull to a stop another hundred yards down the road and blinked its tail lights.

Aaron took out running, trying to figure out what to say when he got there.

He decided to just tell the truth.

As he reached the side of the truck cab, the door swung open and he grabbed the bar and stepped up onto the running board.

"A little late and cool for a hike in the fall with what you're wearing, son, ain't it?"

The guy had to be in his forties at least and was wiry, wearing jeans and a muscle T, with greasy, scraggly hair and probably some missing teeth, although Aaron couldn't be sure in this light. More than a day's growth of stubble and a crude tattoo on a well-worked bicep. Not Aaron's normal choice of traveling companion, but Aaron couldn't be choosy.

"Sorry. I'm from the college in Milbank. We headed in the right direction? And, sorry. I'm out here on a fraternity pledge hazing. I was brought out here and dumped on the side of the road."

"I'se always goin' in the right direction, son. Fraternity, you say? So you're one of those hotsie tottsy college frat guys then?"

"Yes, sorry. Is it OK if I hitch a ride with you into town?"

"We'll see about that. We'll see what sort of arrangement we can make."

Aaron hopped up into the cab and settled on the seat beside the driver. He was desperate to get off the road at this time of night. The sound of the gravel behind him had spooked him. The driver put the rig in gear and slowly eased back up onto the road. He picked up speed rapidly.

"Thanks," Aaron said as they got under way. "I don't have my wallet or anything. If you get me back to my frat house, I can pay you something. Or if you don't want to go out of your way, I'll just get off wherever our paths diverge."

"Paths diverge. That's a good one." The driver laughed. "They teach you those kind of words in college, do they?"

"Yeah, I guess," Aaron said, trying his best to stay on the driver's good side. "So, is it OK? Seeing that I wasn't left with anything I could pay you with now."

"Oh, I think you have something you can pay me with."

"Uhh."

"I ain't been sucked by a college fraternity guy this week. So how would that be in payment?" The driver laughed again, as if he'd made an award-winning joke.

"Uhh. Sorry. Just stop and I'll get out."

"You want out, you can just open the door and jump." Another spat of laughter; another sterling joke.

The semi was going something over the fifty-five-mile speed limit already.

"Them guys didn't just dump you out there, did they? Nice young, good-lookin' piece of ass like you. You had to give 'em something first, dinna ya?"

Aaron looked over sharply at the man. How could he know that? Country yokel like that.

"Why? Why are you talking like that?" Aaron asked, the distress cutting through in his voice.

"Oh, maybe jus' the devil gettin' in me. Maybe it's 'cause I ain't got none in nearly a thousand miles and seein' you near naked like that made me randy. Why else would I've a stopped? You gotta know what truckers usually want from hitchhikers. 'Specially in the middle of the night out in the countryside. So, what's it to be? Leavin' me at sixty or givin' me a blow job and getting' door to door service to the college?"

The driver had already unzipped himself and pulled a plump cock out. He was steering with one hand and fisting his cock with the other.

"Here? Now? While you're driving?"

"Sure. I could handle this rig in my half sleep while humpin' a slut's cunt. Ain't like I never did it before, son. I'se a professional driver. In more ways than one." Another brilliant joke, and the driver was laughing his head off again at his talent.

Aaron sighed and leaned over and took the cock in his hand and lowered his lips to the tip. The driver was right. It wasn't like he hadn't done this himself before—not even the first time tonight. He didn't have a whole lot of choices. He had to get back to the college somehow. Boy did he owe those fraternity brothers for this, though.

The driver gave him no warning that he was going to come, so Aaron took much of what he had down his throat. He gagged a bit, but then he sat back up on his side of the cab and ran a forearm across his mouth to wipe away the shame of it.

"See that, Cal?" the driver said over his shoulder. "Got a good look at that? Frat guy gave good head, did'n he?"

"Yep. Saw it all," a gruff voice answered from behind the seats. Aaron jerked his head back and looked between the seats and saw for the first time that there was a cubicle behind there. It was pitch dark, but he could make out a large hairy shape. The flesh he could see told him the guy back there was naked or near enough.

"Really turned me on, Irv," The voice said. "Pullin' on myself back here. Ready for my turn."

"OK, go ahead. Then you can relieve me, and I can get my nuts off proper."

Aaron reached for the door handle, ready to leap, speeding semi or no speeding semi. But the guy in the back was too fast for him. Aaron was wrapped in strong, beefy, hairy arms and pulled into the cubicle behind the seats. He could see little other than a pudgy, grinning face, but he could smell the man's foul, tobacco-sour breath, and he could hear his heavy breathing. He felt helpless as he was manhandled and fondled and controlled. And he felt the pain and filling of the guy's cock in his channel, after he'd been wedged into the back corner of the cubicle with the small of his back on a padded cushion, his pelvis rolled up, and his legs forcibly spread, with the heel of one shoe wedged against the back of the seat he'd been sitting in and the other dug into a hold bar at the back of the cubicle and near its ceiling.

The unseen assailant stroked him hard and fast and came quickly, Aaron thankful at least that he was wearing a condom.

"Finished," a voice croaked between heavy breathing. "Pull over for a minute and we'll change positions."

Irv, the driver, was more practiced and proficient and took his own sweet time, as he needed time to reload from Aaron's blow job earlier. He also was more insistent on Aaron pleasing him and taking several positions that taxed Aaron more than any of the other encounters he'd had that night.

Aaron was nearly comatose when the rig was pulled over to the side of the road again, and he was pushed out of the cab and landed hard in the scrub beside the road, his shorts in his mouth, where Irv had stuffed them when Aaron had become so vocal when Irv was at the height of what he had to give Aaron.

After the rig pulled off, Aaron lay, bruised and cut at the side of the road and just sobbed. He looked down the road. The lights on the horizon didn't look any closer than when he'd gotten in the semi. He was as abandoned and alone out here as he'd ever been. In a jerky motion, wanting to do something to respond to his feeling of violation and humiliation, he rose painfully and drew on his athletic shorts. It wasn't much. It was the best he could do to achieve whatever dignity that was left to him.

He was angry and frustrated. And he was more angry at his fraternity brothers than at Irv and Cal. His resentment of them, strangely, was more a matter of not living up to their bargain and returning him to town than in assaulting him. He'd been fucked so many times tonight, that what they took from him seemed to have little importance at this point. But his fraternity brothers. They had done this to him. Boy did he want them to pay.

* * * *

"Are you OK? Do you need a lift somewhere?" The voice was rich and silky and, for some reason, filled Aaron with relief. He looked up. He'd been so worked up that he hadn't seen the sleek, black limousine glide up beside him and stop. The rear passenger door was open, and the voice reached out from the interior to enfold and caress him.

But Aaron couldn't reply. He was on the verge of tears again, whether it was from frustration and anger and hopelessness or from relief he couldn't say.

"You need help, I can see. And you need to get home. You should not be out here like this at night. And you're hurt. You need comfort. Come into the car, and I will take care of you."

Aaron felt his feet move, and he was climbing into the backseat of the limousine. As soon as he clicked the door shut, the limousine's engine purred and the vehicle slid out onto the road. It was only a short distance up the road that they came to a crossover, and the vehicle did a smooth, almost floating, U-turn onto the other side of the road and moved back toward where they'd come from.

"Uh. I need to go to the college. To Milbank."

"Milbank is in this direction," the voice purred. "Don't worry. We will see you home."

Aaron turned and looked across the seat into the darkness. His traveling companion was wrapped in a cloak and the dark shadows. Aaron only had the sensation of sharp features, dark complexion, a black goatee of a beard, and piercing eyes. He looked away from the eyes. He had the sensation that when they made eye contact, the figure in the corner held him in thrall. Hands appeared from inside the cloak—moving as the figure spoke in a soothing, melodic baritone. The fingers of the hands were slender and long, the nails well manicured and especially long for a man—and seemed to be filed into points.

The fingers were feminine, but the voice masculine. Aaron was confused.

"How did you . . . ?"

"How did I what, Aaron?"

Aaron was nonplused. "I don't understand."

"It's enough now that I understand, Aaron. I understand all about you. I know you as no other person knows you. And I know what has happened to you this night."

"You know?" Aaron asked in a hushed whisper. "Who? How? Why are you here?"

"I am here because you summoned me, Aaron. I did not know you were capable of it. I'd never thought you might be one."

"I . . . I don't understand," Aaron croaked. He was beaten and fucked and totally exhausted. And now this. He was completely out of his element.

"No you're not, not really," the voice said.

"I'm not what?"

"Out of your element. I'm as surprised as you are. But there you have it. And here we are. And it looks like we can do business."

"Business? What in the hell are you talking about?" Aaron was angry now. Anger on top of confusion and frustration.

"See, you do have it in you," the voice said. And then there was a low, self-satisfied laugh. "If your fraternity brothers were here in front of you now and you had the power, you would make them suffer utter damnation, wouldn't you?"

"Yes," Aaron blurted out.

"And, so, that's why we're here, why our paths have crossed. I specialize in utter damnation. For just a small consideration, I can give you all the revenge you want."

"You can . . . ? What sort of shit is this? Is this part of the pledge hazing?"

"No, not at all, Aaron. This is part of your revenge. If you are interested . . . and if you are willing to pay the price."

"Interested? Price? I don't believe . . ."

"Yes you do, Aaron. Deep, down inside you believe. You summoned me. And you are willing to pay the price. I know that even if you don't yet. That's why I'm here. That's why when you summoned me, I came."

"I summoned you? This is ridiculous."

A heavy sigh was emitted from the darkened corner. "You certainly run deep, don't you? Such self-delusion. You need convincing. Here. You have cuts and bruises. Here, lean over toward me."

Aaron's eyes opened wide as the cloak parted and the man—no, the beast—leaned in to him and a long, forked tongue flicked out of his mouth. More of Aaron's attention was going to what else he could see, though: a swarthy complexion and trails of hair down a naked chest. Pointed ears, small horns at the temple. A centered, impossibly long, slender cock curved up from four heavy balls. The trail of chest and belly hair descending to fully pelted goat's legs and ending in cloven feet.

How in the hell did the fraternity guys manage this, was Aaron's dominant thought. And he thought he might laugh, but he was shaking too badly to do so. Thus, the only sound that came out of him initially was a frightened snort. "The devil you . . ." he then whispered huskily.

"Yes, precisely. Hold still. This won't hurt. You will enjoy this, and it will bring you relief—and, I think, understanding and acceptance. I'm not here to hurt you; I'm here to fulfill your wants."

Aaron leaned away from the monster, laying down on his back on the wide seat, but paralyzed, immobile to the hands that closed over his arms under his biceps and the warm, naked body that covered him and to the tongue and lips that moved to his body, sliding from bruise to cut, which cleared up instantly under the attention of the caresses of the monster's mouth.

Aaron couldn't move, not only from the horror of it but also from the comfort and sensuous healing touch of the devil's lips and tongue—and the warmth of his body and the silken caress of his body hair on Aaron's flesh. When he was done bringing Aaron's broken and cut body back to the height of rosy health, the devil's lips descended on Aaron's cock, and Aaron laid back and enjoyed a more sensuous and complete blow job than he'd ever had from a mortal.

When the devil finished draining Aaron dry, he sat up and released his hold on Aaron and said, "Do you believe me now?"

"No . . . yes, how could I not? But I . . ."

"I'm here because of what happened to you tonight—in fact because of what the man you trusted led you in to. And because of the power of your frustration and humiliation and anger. You want revenge for that, don't you?"

"Yes," Aaron whispered. There was no use hiding this. The devil certainly knew it. It was time that he admitted it to himself. "But at what cost?" Aaron asked.

"Why, your soul, of course," and the devil laughed like the answer was obvious. "Don't you read your folklore?"

"Yes, but how, what . . . ?"

"I must possess you. Possess you fully. But in turn, you will be quite pleased with your life. After tonight that shouldn't be either misunderstood by you or all that difficult. Do you understand?"

"Yes, yes, I guess I do," Aaron answered.

"And you are prepared for that?" the devil asked?

What else was there for Aaron to say? After what he'd already been through that night. Knowing what he wanted to do about it.

"Come here," the devil said as he sat back up and he held out his hand.

The fucking was divine. No pain, and the sensation of deep, filling completion. Again and again. The devil drew Aaron onto his lap, facing away from him, the devil's arms completely encasing him. And Aaron was fucked just the way he had hoped that Jack would fuck him earlier in the evening, in their room, before the hazing started.

But Aaron had no illusions. He knew that Jack could never fuck him like this. Jack would never touch him so deeply, stretch his channel so fully, pump him so long and completely, fill him to the overflow with sweet, calming nectar. He would never set Aaron on fire. Again and again and again.

When the devil had come deep inside him, filling Aaron with a pleasure and calmness he'd never experienced before, the devil murmured, "Was that a price too high to pay?"

"Not unless it was given to me just that once and will now be a solitary memory."

Pleased at the response, the devil whispered, "That need not be. I require no waiting time." And once more Aaron was lying on his back along the seat, with his legs parted and hooked on top of the devil's hairy, bulbous buttocks, and the devil was on top of him, making Aaron moan and sigh at the heat of the devil's body and the feel of the silken hair on his body, and moving deeper, deeper inside him. And the slender cock was thickening into a mighty pole of taking, stripping Aaron of his very soul—with Aaron crying out, begging for the devil to take more of him—no matter the cost.

* * * *

Alert and smiling and on time, Aaron aced his chemistry exam the next day—and all of his exams and papers after that as well.

Bert was the first one to leave the fraternity—and the college, followed almost immediately by Tom. Bert, the brilliant student, was caught cheating on an exam—and was turned in by Tom. Bert was dismissed from the school. When he was called to task, he just hung his head and said, "The devil made me do it." The school administrators weren't impressed or amused. No more impressed and amused was the fraternity counsel when Tom was

65

called on the carpet for snitching on a senior brother and gave the same "the devil made me do it" reply in defense. He was hounded out of the frat house and the college forthwith.

Pete was caught trying to steal a case of beer in open daylight from a grocery store near the college campus. He was looking glazed and muttering, "The devil made me do it," as he was hauled off to the goal, complaining that of course he didn't steal the beer of his own will; his family had access to all of the beer they could possibly want.

A special place in hell was reserved for Jack, when Pete went to trial and identified Jack as his accomplice in the crime. That same day, before he could be arrested, Jack slipped on his own sweat on the basketball court and came down hard on the floor, shattering his kneecap. He would never be able to play basketball again, but the loss of his scholarship and his planned professional sports career were made moot by his arrest. In the holding cell, he beat up Pete badly, mad as he was that the only reason Pete would give for implicating him was that the devil had made him do it—and this act sent Jack to prison, where he became the favorite of all of the prisoners who hadn't had the privilege of going to college and playing competitive basketball.

Aaron was most pleased at the sendoff for smart ass ringleader Tony. The fraternity was already dissolving around their ears and Aaron had moved in with another guy in a nice apartment closer to the college, when Tony was pulled out of the burning fraternity house, naked and holding the lighter he'd used to torch all of the draperies in the house. The house went up in flames nicely, seeming to enjoy the flash sendoff from the indignities it had gone through. When Tony's angry father showed up and watched his investment go up in flames and turned on his son, all Tony could say was "The devil made me do it," with a big-ass grin on his face. A disgusted father refused to cover Tony's bail, and Tony was given the undivided amorous attention of three bikers on four successive nights in holding before he crawled into his arraignment.

By then, though, Sam, the football star, and Aaron were humming along swimmingly in their new love nest apartment. Sam worshiped the ground that Aaron walked on. He took care of all of the domestic chores and bedded Aaron every night just as

Aaron liked it—that was every night that Aaron wasn't off renewing his soul sale to the figure in the backseat of the sleek black limousine.

Curse of the Tan Tan

"Oh, Philippe. OH, Philippe!" The dark, handsome young Moroccan had been murmuring Philip's name when the American adventurer had started rimming him but was now crying his name out insistently as Philip split his curvaceous butt cheeks with his hard, throbbing cock and thrust down, once, twice, three times. "Philippe!" the Moroccan exclaimed and writhed under him with each deep thrust.

He was very good. The Moroccan bottom was very, very good—nicely formed and well-muscled, but willowy and compliant and with a boyish charm that was almost beyond handsome. Deep bronze skin, black curly hair, and fluttery eyelashes. His big brown eyes had a well-practiced "being taken for the first time, noncompliantly" look to them that was tantalizing to Philip. The exclamations of his name in French were very arousing to the American as well—a very, very nice added touch.

And the American was accustomed to having the best. The two young hunks were spread out on the wide, pillow-strewn bed in an executive suite of the Marrakech Millennium Hotel. The two had met for drinks in the swankiest bar Marrakech could provide, had eaten in one of the best restaurants in all of northern Africa, and had then moved to Philip's suite at one of the top hotels in the world, where Philip had quickly stripped Harun down, pushed him down on the bed on his belly, strapped his wrists to the headboard with leather bonds, and begun taking him hard and rough. This had been fine with Harun, although he could form no real affection for this selfish, demanding American.

Everything had been prearranged. The American was accustomed to the best of everything, and Harun had been engaged from the best male brothel in the city.

"Philippe, O-h-h, Philippe!" Harun moaned, as Philip straddled his hips from above, a knee beside one hip and his foot planted firmly beside the opposite hip, as he fucked down into the Moroccan sideways from above. Philip liked unusual positions. And he was a connoisseur of sex. He had fucked like this all over the world. But this Harun was proving to be one of the best and most arousing.

"Call me Philippe again," Philip whispered in a low, lust-choked voice. "I love it when you speak French to me like that."

"Oh, Philippe, Philippe, *mon amour*. O-H-H!"

Nearly an hour later Philip was reclined on his back on the bed and the lithe, flexible Moroccan was stretched out, belly up, on top of him, moving ever so slowly and languidly on top of the golden-blond, studiously muscled American stud. Philip had his pelvis plastered to Harun's pert buttocks and his cock was still churning deep inside the talented call boy. Harun's hands were now bound together and his arms were flung back so that his wrists rested on the back of Philip's neck, stretching his boyish torso out fully. He had his heels dug into the bed and his pelvis lifted a bit so that Philip could thrust up into him. He was still moaning and groaning as if Philip was splitting him asunder, and, indeed, Philip had a tool that had that effect on most men.

Both men climaxed and Harun lowered himself onto Philip to rest, with the American still deeply encased inside him. Philip had the palms of his hands firmly planted on the Moroccan's nipples and was nuzzling Harun's neck with his lips and teeth, nipping at the young man's throat to the point of nearly drawing blood. This was slightly painful for Harun, but he was a professional and the American had paid a small fortune for his attentions—or, at least, had arranged to pay for him. Harun suffered far worse at the pleasure of the local, more demanding and stingy clients on a weekly basis.

Harun whispered above the sucking noises at his neck. "But I do not know why you tell me of this, Philippe, *mon amour.* This is something it is not wise to be mentioning at all in Marrakech. The Dakar Rally and its integrity are taken very seriously here in Morocco."

"I have money," Philip said with almost a pout in his voice, as if taking for granted that money solved all problems. "All I want is for someone to take me and the Beast on the rally route for this year so I have a feel for how the course is. This is my first year. Some of the drivers have been doing this for years; they already know all about the conditions."

"But this time of year," Harun said insistently. "This is the worst possible time to be out in the desert in a vehicle. The Sirocco. It is . . ."

"I know all about the winds that rush across northern Africa and into Spain and France at this time of year," Philip said with a snort. He wasn't used to being opposed like this. Philip's father could buy Morocco if he wanted to. All Philip wanted was someone to guide him on the off-road vehicle rally course in anticipation of this year's dash from Lisbon to Dakar, Senegal, across the Sahara and down the western coast of northern Africa. And he knew there were rules against driving the course beforehand. That's why it was important to do so now, when the threat of the Sirocco winds kept prying eyes out of the desert quadrant. Philip had spent millions on the technology that had gone into the Beast. He had to win the race. And to do that, he needed to have a leg up on the others on the course.

"I'm sorry, it just isn't possible," Harun said, punctuating the "isn't" to end the conversation. He didn't mind getting fucked by this spoiled American; in fact, he rather enjoyed it. But he was a city sophisticate. The Dakar Rally was nothing to him other than a periodic jump in the client pool numbers.

"I'm sure there's someone on the street willing to guide me," Philip said stubbornly. "I will pay very well."

"If you go out on the street looking for this someone, you are sure to either be arrested quickly or get in with someone who will take you out into the desert and slit your . . . pay well, you say? Just how well?"

Harun had just realized how many dirhams the brothel would be paid for his services this evening, more than a month's usual salary in his share alone. And such a waste. The American was so handsome and well built that if Harun had met him by chance in the bar, he would have come back to the hotel with him for free. Of course, the man would have had to keep silent during the fuck then. Harun could hardly bear his arrogance and self-possession. But the American was throwing money and IOUs around like he had no idea of their value. And as Harun had already noted to himself, the Dakar Rally was nothing to him. He didn't care about its integrity or its rules.

"I'll pay $100,000 U.S. to the man who guides me and the Beast through the course to Dakar," Philip responded in a blustery voice.

There was a period of silence while Harun contemplated and Philip slow fucked and chewed on Harun's neck.

"I'll take you there," Harun said at length in a quiet voice. "For that money, I'll take you there myself . . . but how did your vehicle get that name?"

Philip laughed, happy now that he was getting his way. But, then, he always got his way. Money always won out. He pushed Harun up and off of him and waggled his baseball bat of a cock with his fist. He then turned Harun back onto his stomach. "I named it after this. I named it after my cock. The

Beast. I plan on fucking the competition in this running of the race."

And then Philip demonstrated once again why his cock was called the Beast, as he reversed himself above Harun, stretched out on his belly, and, once more pelvis to buttocks, but now Philip's hard, beefy calves encasing the sides of Harun's chest and his hands wrapped around Harun's ankles, Philip began pumping the ass of the Moroccan prostitute-turned-road companion and guide again. Harun writhed and groaned in genuine ecstasy under him.

"Philippe, oh, oh, Philippe," Harun was crying out. "PHILLIPE!"

* * * *

Three days later, as they approached the southern Morocco town of Tan Tan, where the desert dunes met the Atlantic Ocean coastline, the Sirocco hit them in a swirl of dust that obliterated their whole world. They literally couldn't see more than two feet beyond the dust-caked windscreen of the Beast.

"Quick, pull in over there. Over there, where we saw the ruins of a large compound before the Sirocco descended," Harun yelled above the whining of the dust-laden wind.

"Time. We don't have the time," Philip yelled back. "We're two hours behind my calculations of a winning pace. We must press ahead."

"We can't possibly keep going," Harun screamed back. "You can just subtract the down time from your calculations. The engine will quickly clog in this dust storm. The dust will get into everything." And in fact, both of the men were already covered with dust even though the Beast was locked down as tight as a ship.

"No worries," Philip retorted with bravado and a grin. "This is a multimillion dollar machine. This has been designed for any . . ." The grin slid right off Philip's face, as a painful clanking and wheezing sound wafted up from the engine compartment of the Beast.

"Quick, as I said," Harun persisted. "The vehicle—and we as well—need to get under cover immediately. There, there. Drive in that direction. Now! Oh, God, what was that?"

Philip had turned the wheel and headed in the direction Harun had pointed, but just as they saw a crumbling mud-brick wall and an opening big enough for the Beast to fit through, there was a swirl of something black and enveloping across the windscreen and the sensation of a flash of white fangs. Something was out here with them. Or so it seemed. But it was over in a flash. And whatever it was, it was as much beleaguered by the sudden Sirocco as they were.

Harun was stunned at the visitation—longer certainly than Philip was, who was moving on to reacting to each new problem assaulting him in his attempt to maneuver the Beast to safety.

When they had gotten through the opening in the outer wall, they were in luck. This was some kind of fortress from ages past. There were still some buildings standing with roofs on and openings on the side away from the direction of the Sirocco wind for them to pull the Beast in, under cover, and then for they themselves to grab blankets and some provisions and retreat beyond doorways with doors they could close. From the entrance, they were able to escape through a series of rooms to a sufficiently sheltered space to hold back the Sirocco.

It was dark in the room they finally entered, but only because the Sirocco had blackened the sky. There were several rents in the crumbling wall, which, luckily was set away from the wind, so that the room would be lighted well on a normal day. They had a battery lantern with them, though, so Philip wasn't worried about the dark—at least for now, for as long as the batteries held.

When Philip looked up from spreading the blankets and fussing with the provisions they had brought in, he saw that Harun was nervously pacing back and forth from one end of the small room to the other. Harun obviously was worried about something.

"It's fine," Philip said. "I've read up on the Sirocco. At this time in the season, this should let up in a couple of hours.

74

A few hours and we can be on our way again. And we're almost to Laayuoune. We can reprovision there."

"I only noticed, from the signs on the walls in the rooms we passed through to get here, where we are," Harun said. And there was something dread-based in Harun's voice that made a chill run down Philip's spine.

"What are you saying? Where are we?"

"I live in the city now, but I was raised near here. I have heard the legends. This is an old French Foreign Legion post," Harun said. "We're actually on a cliff overlooking the sea. The legion was here because piracy was rampant here at one time. The trade route goes right through here, and the pirates would land just long enough to snatch their fill of goods and slaves and be off on the sea again. And then they often sailed into the arms of other pirates awaiting them just over the horizon. There are several burned hulls of ships washed up on the rocks below this cliff."

"Yes, so?" Philip asked.

"So, there are legends about this place," Harun said. "The post was well manned, but one season it suddenly became deserted."

"Deserted?" Philip snorted. "So where did all the legionnaires go?"

"That's just it," Harun responded, and there was fear in his voice. "The villagers in Tan Tan had been having trouble with wolves, or so they claimed. Some of the villagers were found dead, their throats torn open and their bodies ravaged. But then their local magic men—we call them *fuqaha* and you call them witch doctors—had the villagers stay close to the village and the village lighted with great bonfires day and night, and the problem stopped, at least down there."

"Stopped?" Philip asked with a superior tone of disbelief. "Just like that? For how long?"

"Well, forever," Harun said. "Because they are still doing it, still keeping their village well lit, and their elders are still chanting incantations to what they claim is the devil. The legend is that strong. Men have continued to disappear from the village from time to time, but while the slave boats were passing, that was ascribed to the pirates or to warriors from nearby villages. And now when it happens, they just assume the men have been blinded by the promise of the big city lights and have gone to seek their fortunes. But legend was reinforced by what happened here in this fortress."

"What happened here?" Philip asked. He was toying with Harun now, mocking him. The man claimed to be a city sophisticate, but you scratch a North African and they will go native on you in a flash.

"No one knows. Although . . . although . . ." Harun barely could go on. The here, now, this deserted post and the legend of it were merging. "As I noted, some say this is the work of the devil," he whispered. He stood there, breathing heavily before he could muster the fortitude to go on. "There were thirty men or more in the legion unit here, but one day, when none of the legionnaires had come into Tan Tan to drink and fuck for some time, a few of the villagers were brave enough to come up here—but they found the place deserted."

"The devil? Sheer superstition. No doubt they just found the drink and prostitutes more palatable up in Goulimine and then found it was too long a distance to go back and forth and just deserted en masse," Philip said with a laugh. But then he went on. "You say there was no accounting for what could have happened to them?"

"Well, there is the cliff and many skeletons have washed up on the rocks below. But it would be unthinkable that thirty strong men would all have fallen off the cliff to their deaths below in just one season. And where there are ancient ship hulks washing up on the rocks, there are sure to be skeletons as well. Whatever it was, the villagers below and the legionnaires up here did not get along at all. The villagers claimed the legionnaires preyed on them—and especially on their young women and men. And now they don't. And the villagers claim it's because they discovered how to summon the devil."

"A version of the big city lights as opposed to the dreariness of the foreign legion life sounds the most plausible to me," Philip said with a sniff. He was fiddling with the lantern now. The light had dimmed. They might be in the dark soon.

"Shush. Did you hear that?" Harun said with a tremulous voice.

"Hear what?" Philip asked absentmindedly. He had turned to bunching up blankets on the uneven dirt floor and testing to see how hard the ground was. He had unbuttoned his shirt and stripped it off.

"It sounded like some sort of animal—a howl of some sort."

"I didn't hear it. And there's something I want to do now. Something I've pledged good money for and haven't had since Goulimine. And I have no intention of going into Tan Tan for it in this dust storm, either. So, get your sweet little ass over here. I paid for your ass." Philip stood and unzipped his pants.

For the next three-quarters of an hour, Harun's mind was completely absorbed by something other than the devil and the disappearance of the legionnaires, as he spent much of the time rolled up onto his shoulders with his buttocks up in the air, while Philip crouched over him, his thighs pressing in on the Moroccan's hips and his cock jackhammering down into Harun's ass canal. The American was paying well, so Harun writhed and whined and moaned for him. It wasn't long though before the Moroccan's grunts and bleatings were genuine. The American was an expert in what he did so well—and he could be very cruel.

When Philip pulled out of him and they were lying side by side, Harun raised a question that had been worrying him.. "You said that you were depositing a large advance on my pay in the bank before we left Marrakech. But nothing was there when we left. Had you forgotten?"

"You can wait for your pay until this job is done," Philip growled.

"You are going to pay me, aren't you?" Harun asked. He tried to keep the plaintive tone out of his voice. He suddenly felt vulnerable.

"You're lucky if I don't turn you in to the authorities when we return—for prostitution and for urging me to take this test run while holding from me that it was illegal. Or that's certainly what I could claim, and I'm sure the authorities would believe me over you." Philip laughed and slapped Harun on the butt. "But enough of this. You should pay me for the cocking you get. Turn over. I feel like dipping into your honey pot again."

When Philip had had his satisfaction, Harun took a towel and a canteen of water and slipped out of the room, saying he'd find some corner to relieve himself in and get cleaned up a bit.

Philip busied himself with eating some of the delicacies he'd packed and checking over the maps to familiarize himself with the next leg of their journey. The light from the lantern was growing dimmer and dimmer. Philip hoped the Sirocco would give up its grip on them soon.

He had no idea how long he'd been amusing himself before he realized that it seemed a long time since Harun had left. After several more minutes, even though the light was nearly gone, Philip had recharged his own batteries and felt like another fuck, so he went looking for Harun.

They were three rooms away. Philip was so surprised by what he saw that he stood there, dumbly for the longest time, trying to figure out what he was looking at.

It seemed to be a large square of black silk mounded over something in the middle of the room and undulating up and down, the cloth rippling out from the center to the sides.

He must have made some sort of guttural noise, because the cloth suddenly rose up higher and swirled as a monstrous figure turned toward him. It was both man and beast. It had to be at least seven feet tall. The black material, which proved to be a cape, swirled away from the body of the man beast as it turned, snorted, and eyed Philip with great interest. It was the shape of a man, at least from the waist up, but everything about it was exaggerated, the whole musculature—big and bulging and plump, a veritable champion of champions among body builders—right down to the most monstrous cock and bulbous, low-hanging balls— four of them—that Philip had ever seen. The beast was hairy, black curly hair trailing down its torso and then into heavy matting on its goat legs, which ended in cloven feet. Half man at least, but almost to the point of identifying as nonhuman.

But, no, it was definitely a man. All man—the cock and balls screaming its maleness. And its face was malevolence itself. Not ugly—in fact, pointed-chin handsome in a wild, rugged way. Goateed and with pointed ears and the nubs of horns at its temples. But the eyes were red, blood shot, and the flashing teeth were white and sharp, with pronounced fangs . . . and they were dripping in blood.

That's when Philip noticed that the beast wasn't alone. The cape had been covering not only the beast. Harun, but a pale and diminished Harun, was lying there under the beast's crouched body. Harun's legs were spread wide and the beast had been kneeling there between Harun's thighs. The Moroccan prostitute was white as a sheet and wasn't moving. He, in fact, looked entirely drained of life. The beast had a huge hand under Harun's buttocks, holding his pelvis up, and it was obvious that the beast had been fucking Harun when Philip appeared. Harun's head was lolled over to the side at an awkward angle, and his blood-covered neck was arched and exposed. His eyes were open and glazed, but there was a wan smile on his face as if he had supremely enjoyed whatever had happened to him.

A moment of sniffing each other out, and then the beast gave Philip a languid, very-pleased-with-itself look and almost nonchalantly pushed the head of its dick into Harun's yawning hole and slowly, ever so slowly, made every inch of its cock disappear.

Philip was panting hard and giving little gasps as he saw that huge cock slowly disappear inside the hole he had so recently been splitting himself. The beast smiled, eyes intently and warily watching Philip as Philip's eyes were glued on that huge tool moving slowly, deliberately, in and out. A flow of semen, much too full a flow for a normal man, was seeping out of Harun's hole each time the mushroom cap appeared, only to descend again in the slick lubrication of the beast's own cum. Whenever the mushroom cap slurped out of the hole, Philip could see a steady stream of white cum dribbling down from the slit. There was no reaction from Harun. He was slumped over, collapsed into himself.

Philip and the beast were suspended in some sort of standoff. The beast seemed content with its total taking of Harun as long as Philip stood there in rigid shock. Philip broke the silence and disrupted the tableau first by screaming and then by turning and running for the inner chamber. He'd brought a gun into the fort. All he could think of was that he needed to reach that gun.

The beast was loping behind him and gaining ground. Philip could hear its snuffling and heavy panting quick on his heels, and he had barely reached the door into the inner chamber, when his ankle was gripped and his body came crashing to the ground. He continued as best he could, dragging himself toward the center of the room, the adrenaline pumping and moving him forward, toward the satchel where he'd put the gun. And the beast was crawling up his back, covering his body inch by inch, ripping at the clothes he'd loosely draped back on his body after fucking Harun, with its nails and teeth, stripping him naked.

Philip collapsed on the ground under the weight of the beast when he was just a few feet away from the satchel. He stretched out his hand and felt the leather of the satchel. But he saw a long, heavily muscled, hairy arm reach up and a strong fist closing around his wrist, and he was being pulled back.

Fully covering Philip's back, the beast wrapped its arms around Philip's chest and stomach and was pulling him up onto his knees, hugging Philip's shoulder blades into its hunky pecs, holding Philip close to its chest. A hand went down to Philip's belly and then on down and took a firm grip under Philip's exposed balls and pulled Philip's hips upward along its own heaving belly.

Philip screamed as he felt the size of the beast's gigantic mushroom cap at the entrance of his ass canal, and then he cried and moaned, "No, no, no," as the beast brought him slowly down and down and down onto the semen-slicked monster tool, impaling his ass canal on an impossibly long and thick—and well-lubricated—cock.

The beast had Philip entirely under its control now. Philip's ass was skewered firmly on its cock and its arms held the American close to its chest. They were erect, on their knees, but the beast was able to slide Philip up and down on its torso at will. The beast was simply too big and strong for the pampered American. Philip, arms flailing until they became too heavy and just hung down his side, gasped and groaned and heaved and panted and cried out as he descended on the beast's throbbing manhood. But the beast was almost gentle now. It was pulling Philip onto its sword slowly, making an effort to let Philip stretch as best he could, and it was nuzzling Philip's neck with its mouth, giving him a long kiss there on the throbbing artery stretching down his neck, just under the surface of the skin. A kiss of lips and tongue and then teeth.

The teeth. The teeth. It felt like only pin pricks, but increasingly Philip felt the sucking sensation, the feeling of flowing. His blood, flowing out of him. Draining from him.

The beast was making a low humming sound, a soothing sound—almost a lullaby tune. Enjoying its feeding in every way. And, having bottomed out and given Philip's passage walls an opportunity to stretch to its needs, the beast began lifting and lowering Philip on that massive cock. The black silk cape was rippling around the two of them, caressing Philip's bare arms and shoulders. One of the beast's large hands encased one of Philip's pecs, and a thumb and forefinger were applying and releasing pressure on a nipple to match the rhythm of the gentle fucking and sucking. The beast's other palm was on Philip's lower belly, holding the young American close to him, and long sensuous fingers stretched to either side of Philip's cock and applying rhythmic pressure to veins at the base of Philip's cock that caused him to harden and ejaculate quickly and then harden quickly again and ejaculate again.

For the first time in his life, Philip did not have control. He was being played and drained. Completely defenseless and becoming increasingly so.

Philip was losing interest in escaping. The fuck was glorious, and he was growing weaker and more disoriented, but, at the same time, rising in arousal. The beast was filling him, deep, with one long, flowing ejaculation. And Philip's own cock was being milked again and again with great expertise and satisfaction.

Philip's head lolled to one side. He was loving the feeling of the flowing of the blood from him to the beast; he felt like they were one, supreme, well-oiled fucking unit. If he could think about it he'd have known why Harun had the silly, satiated smile on his face. On and on the beast was fucking up into him, reaching new depths with each slow pump. And flowing. Not a single, jerky cum shot spouting, but a flowing of warming essences. Philip's blood was being exchanged with a flowing of numbing semen.

The young American was drifting off, and he was doing so with only the mild regret that he might not be able to feel the full effect of the total, possessing fuck if he lost consciousness.

But then there was a howling screech, and a tearing sensation at both throat and ass as the beast lurched and jerked this way and that and pulled out of and away from Philip and went racing out of the room in an awkward, bent-over lope with a deafening scream. Philip just collapsed on the floor, too tired and drained to move. But his eyes flitted open . . . to find that the room was now bathed in light streaming in from the chinks in the crumbling walls.

Philip lay there for some time, maybe even hours. He had no idea how long he was there. He only knew that slowly, slowly his strength was coming back to him. He managed to drag himself to the center of the room and eat and drink from the provisions he'd brought in. And, eventually, he was able to stand and to walk. He gathered up the satchel, remembering to fumble around and extract the gun he'd placed there.

Then, holding the gun in front of him with a trembling hand, he tentatively moved out of the room. He instinctively moved from one well-lit spot to the next, not even consciously knowing why, just knowing somehow that that was an important thing for him to do. He could see his vehicle, the Beast, under its cover when he emerged from the building. He didn't fully comprehend what it was at first, but he slowly fixated on the knowledge that the Beast was his salvation and that they had parked it here for its safety. That's how he thought of it—that "they" had left the Beast there. But he was all muddled now. Who were the "they"? Had he come here with someone or had he come alone? He couldn't quite be clear on that. There certainly was no one else about now. And what had happened? He knew he was incredibly weak, his ass felt like raw hamburger, and his inner thighs felt sticky, but he couldn't fully comprehend what had happened—or how long ago it had happened. Everything was still a hazy blur. Oh, why did he feel so weak?

Something about driving to Dakar, though. He looked at the maps he had with him, and, sure enough, a road was marked that ended in Dakar. Well, he'd just get in the Beast and start driving in that direction. Maybe somewhere down the road his ears would stop ringing and he'd remember more.

But he wasn't even sure he wanted to remember more.

Paulo's Inferno

Paulo was sweating when he placed the listening piece of the telephone back in its cradle. He mopped his brow and loosened the cravat that now seemed to be choking him. He rose and moved to the window wall of his office that looked down into the assembly line factory floor where his firm, what very soon would be his firm, made the sleekest of horseless carriages that now were being called motorcars. Gina had told him just this morning that she feared his ambition and grasping were unbounded and would be his undoing. This after he had ravished her for the third time in as many days, sex mad she had thought until he had let it slip that he could not be assured of his standing in her father's company until they had given the old man a grandson.

He should be pleased now, after the telephone call. Now he need not waste his seed in the acid-tongued Gina anymore. Not if he could trust that smooth, rich-toned voice on the telephone. And he now was far beyond questioning that whoever was behind the voice on the telephone could deliver what was promised.

Three years previously Paulo had been a pimply faced, chubby clerk in a Milan mattress factory, the son of a butcher and dressmaker, destined for nowhere. But then the telephone calls had started. The smooth, rich-toned voice suggesting what he could do to better himself, promising that if he just did this or that or positioned himself here or there or said this or that to a certain person, he would prosper. Paulo had thought the voice had been that of prankster, but whenever he followed through on the suggestions, he found that they actually worked. He joined a men's athletic club and improved his body and looks. He applied for a job in a business in Milan that everyone was laughing about at the time—the development of an invention of a vehicle that could move without being pulled by a horse. And by taking the periodic suggestions telephoned to him by the mysterious voice, he had prospered. Thus, at length he learned not to second guess the voice and just to do as it said, even to the point of asking for the hand of the company owner's daughter. It had been an absurd proposal, or so he thought. But the company owner had seen only what Paulo had developed to, not what Paulo still saw in himself, and the marriage had been settled.

Repeatedly Paulo had asked the voice on the telephone what he wanted, and invariably there had been a little dry laugh and the declaration that the voice only wanted to see Paulo filled with joy for all eternity.

This generous giving by an unseen and unknown benefactor had disturbed Paulo greatly at first, but as he became more handsome and virile and prosperous and successful at everything he did, he came to believe that what he was receiving was only what was due to him. That he deserved this good fortune by right; even that he himself was wholly the source of his success—that perhaps the voice on the telephone was really just his own internal voice of wisdom and superior intelligence.

Paulo became bold and free with himself. He visited prostitutes, at first women, who flattered him and told him how magnificent he was. He believed them. He acquired a mistress, who told him the same thing, that he was the most handsome man she'd ever known and the greatest lover and cocksman she had ever lain under. Paulo began to worship his body as much as his lovers did and to ever more frequently attend his men's club and display himself in all his glory. There were men at the club who expressed the desire to worship Paulo's body too. And Paulo let them. He was an object of superior beauty; he loved himself, and he completely understood that women and other men loved him too and wanted to worship his body, as was only its due.

Men wanted to unite with him, to meld their bodies with his. To enter him and get as close to his perfection as they could. They were passionate for him. And he loved their passion for him and let them make love to his body.

Thus, the telephone call he had just received from the voice should not have come as a shock to him. But it did nonetheless. The voice, in its silky, resonating baritone, had gotten to the heart of his present dilemma.

"You have become disgusted with your Gina, have you not, Paulo? She is ugliness and baseness against your beauty and elegance. You can hardly bear to touch her, is that not true?"

"No, of course not," Paulo said with indignation. And then, because he knew that he could trust the voice and received more when he honestly admitted his most basic needs and wants. "Well, perhaps. But she must be with child—with my child. With a son. Or I shan't have my dream of owning this firm."

"Perhaps. Perhaps not," answered the smooth-toned voice.

"I don't understand," Paulo responded.

"If you impregnate your wife, yes, in time you . . . or your son . . . may inherit the firm. In time, one or the other of you. But there may be a way for you to have the firm immediately in your own right, with no reliance on your wife or her womb."

"A way?" Paulo asked. "What way? You can give me the firm now?"

"Oh, yes, I surely could do that," the voice intoned warmly. And then there was that dry little laugh that sent a shiver up Paulo's spine. "But that's quite a jump, Paulo, quite on a whole new level of our relationship."

"Now? I could have control of the firm now?" Paulo's mouth was fairly salivating.

"Yes, certainly. But for something like this you would have to pledge yourself to me. Do you think you could do that, Paulo?"

"How soon, do you think? Could I have it this year? Next year?"

"You could have it Monday morning, Paulo. Today is Friday. You could have it Monday morning."

Paulo was hooked. "Monday morning," he whispered, and his hands began to tremble and his chest puffed out and his eyes lit up.

"Yes, but you would have to give me Saturday night."

"I don't understand."

"Oh, I think you might. You would have to pledge yourself to me. You would have to come to me in Punta Dufour on Saturday and lay with me for one night, for one night only. And then you would have control of the firm on the next Monday morning that the sun shone on you."

The air went out of Paulo's chest and he collapsed back into the chair and almost dropped the earpiece to the telephone.

"No, no," he stuttered. "I couldn't possibly . . ."

"Of course you could, Paulo. You've lain with men before. I know that and you know that. You have no secrets from me. If you want to be filled with joy eternally, you'll come to me at the Chateau de la Comte Asmodai in Punta Dufour tomorrow night. The firm, Paulo. Think of what you could do with those motor cars. Gina's father is old and is of the old world. Do you really think there will still be a robust firm making motor cars waiting for you when you have given the old man a grandson? If you want to have a firm that competes in making modern motorcars, you must be bold now."

Paulo stood at the window, looking down to the shop floor for the longest time, struggling with himself. The price was too great. It was his own talent and abilities that were propelling him to this phenomenal success, not whatever a mere voice on the telephone was doing on his behalf. He would just get Gina pregnant and the firm would be his.

* * * *

It was a six-hour train ride from Milan up to the Italian alps bordering on Switzerland where the tiny mountain village of Punta Dufour was located. And, of course, Paulo was on the early morning train to the border. It was dark, even though it was still afternoon, when Paulo reached Punta Dufour and stopped at the local tavern for directions to the chateau.

The first question he asked of the jovial tavern keeper concerned the darkness.

"Aye, we live in darkness here, young man," the tavern keeper responded. "Look up there. That would be the Matterhorn that shadows over us. And a beautiful woman she is to encloak us, if I do say myself. And what might be your business in this corner of the world, sir?"

This led to the second question, directions to the Chateau de la Comte Asmodai. The tavern keeper's joviality melted away and he gruffly pointed up at the Matterhorn and told Paulo which of the trails leading up the mountain from the village would take him to the chateau. And with that, the old man withdrew from the bar without so much as offering Paulo an opportunity to buy a drink, and Paulo had to start the journey up the mountain thirsty and on an empty stomach.

He had almost stumbled on the chateau before he even realized it was anywhere in the vicinity. It was wedged into the cliffside just inside a dark ravine and was constructed of the same rock it was sunk in. Still, it was a very imposing building, but it was cold and foreboding.

The man who met Paulo at the door was anything but foreboding, though. He professed not to be the voice on the telephone, but Paulo assumed that his host was only putting up appearances. The young man who ushered Paulo into the chateau and sat him at a table groaning from the weight of delicious-looking food and drink beside a roaring fire in a huge stone fireplace was as beautiful and perfectly formed as a Michelangelo statue. He was blond and blue eyed, in keeping with northern Italian stock, and, although he looked no older than Paulo himself, his conversation revealed an excellent education and a broad experience of the world. And he had a melodious baritone voice that very easily could be identified with that of the voice of the telephone when allowances were made for the rudimentary development of that instrument of communication.

Paulo and his host, who identified himself as Giovanni, conversed with ease and great mutual enjoyment as Paulo feasted from the abundance that had been placed before him. Everything about the interior of the chateau was opulent almost to the point of sensuality, and Paulo quickly warmed to the idea of lying with Giovanni and letting the handsome young man make love to him throughout the night. It appeared that the pledge required for Paulo to have his dreams fulfilled would be a pleasant one. And as he gazed at himself in the various mirrors placed about the room, Paulo knew that lying with him would be a pleasant experience for Giovanni as well.

So absorbed with himself was Paulo that he didn't even notice that, although the mirrors were set at all angles in the room, the only visage to be seen in them was his own.

After Paulo had eaten and Giovanni had offered him brandy in the comfortable chairs before the fire and chatted with him in depth on the intricacies of the new world of auto mechanics while he watched Paulo drink deeply of the brandy, Giovanni led Paulo to a richly appointed bedchamber. There a huge, thick-postered canopied poster bed was positioned in the center of the room on a plush oriental carpet. The bed was draped in heavy, ruby-red damask panels, which Giovanni let down as soon as Paulo had stripped himself on request and settled himself in the bed. The fire had been dying as they had entered the room, and with the drapes drawn around the bed, Paulo was completely enveloped in darkness.

The journey had been long, and he had gorged himself on rich food and strong drink. So, Paulo stretched out on the bed on his belly and quickly dozed off.

He awoke to a tongue flicking along the side of his neck. The thin, but tightly muscled body of another man was reclined on top of him, the man's legs stretched on top of his, and his strong hands holding Paulo's wrists captive in long, sensuous fingers, their thumbs on Paulo's pulse, enabling both lovers to enjoy the ever-more-rapid beat signaling Paulo's arousal.

Paulo's lover was already in full, and prodigious, erection, and his hard cock was curved up under Paulo's ball sack and between his slightly spread thighs.

With visions of Giovanni, Paulo responded to his new-found lover and began to move his body underneath the chest and belly that were closely covering his back. His lover was kissing and sucking at the arteries pumping blood up the side of Paulo's neck, which was sending engorging signals to Paulo's member, and Paulo lifted his pelvis slightly and began stroking the satiny sheets on the bed with his hard tool, slicking them up with his precum.

His lover was humming to him in a resonant baritone as he worked his lips on Paulo's neck and slid his hard, moist cock back and forth between Paulo's buttocks cheeks, sliding up and down, up and down across the rim of Paulo's asshole. Paulo's lover was flowing in precum, which was moving into Paulo's ass channel as the curved cock ran up and down across the hole. Paulo felt the moist lubrication of his lover's desire seeping into his passage, helping to open him up to that monstrous cock.

Paulo was moaning and panting now. He'd never been prepared like this before, his body worshipped like this before. He turned his head, searching for and finding full, sensuous lips—the lips that had attracted him to Giovanni's handsome face. His lover was possessing his mouth with a searching, filling tongue, as sweet tasting as honey.

Paulo lifted his pelvis higher and stroked harder across the slickened surface of the satin sheets. He was pinned to the bed by the ropy chest muscles of a thin but strong torso and by those sensuous fingers of steel at his wrists. The lifting of Paulo's pelvis brought the head of his lover's curved cock squarely on his asshole, and with a slow rotating motion, the cock was entering him, opening him up, stretching him wide and moving into him.

Paulo wanted to scream out in the pain of exquisite passion, but his lover fully possessed his mouth and would not allow him to do so.

Deeper, deeper was he possessed by his lover's cock, which seemed to thicken and length to impossible proportions as it moved into him. Paulo was straining against his imprisonment now, wanting to writhe wildly to this glorious possession, but he was being held fast. He groaned as his passage walls undulated around the sinking cock, and he gasped as he strained at the steely fingers grasping his wrists and burbled his semen across the sheets underneath him in the ecstasy of release. But still his lover moved deeper and wider inside him.

Paulo opened his mouth wide in a silent scream, fully gagged by that sweet-tasting tongue, a tongue that strangely seemed to be forked, as his lover bottomed inside him and with a cry of his own sent his seed spouting deep inside his prey.

It was only then that Paulo realized that something had been switching at his sides and thighs. But before he could focus on this, his lover withdrew his tongue and placed his lips close to Paulo's ear and hissed, "Now you are mine. With this seeding you are fully pledged to me. There is no turning back now."

A chill shot through Paulo's body. His arms were released, although he was still pinned to the bed by his lover's torso and the hard, throbbing cock buried deep inside Paulo's ass. Paulo wildly felt around at his sides and his hands wrapped themselves around a flicking tail.

He turned his body under that of his lover just as flames shot up all around the bed. Not consuming flames, but illuminating flames. Flames that made the world quite clear—a brief, an oh so brief—illumination of a dark, dark world.

He saw his lover for the first time. And the horror of it was overwhelming. His lover was red-skinned, and horned, and he had a long, forked, flicking tail. And his sneering face was fully satanic. He was only half man. His legs, the feeling of silk Paulo had felt against his skin, were those of a goat. And they ended in cloven feet.

"Oh, God," Paulo cried out involuntarily.

"God has absolutely nothing to do with it," the devil cackled with that dry laugh of his.

"But you promised that on Monday . . ."

"I promised you the next Monday that daylight shone on you. You pledged an entire night lying with me," the devil chortled. "And here, in the shadow of the Matterhorn it is always night. And I promised you would be filled with joy eternally."

And then he went off in a gale of laughter. And when he could control himself again, he rolled off to the side of a Paulo immobilized by fear and shock and confusion and pulled his cock out of his prey with a sucking sound and wagged it with his hand.

"And this I call Joy," he said with a cackle. "You have sold yourself to me with your boundless ambition and conceit and, as I promised, I will fill you with Joy for all eternity."

And with that, he rolled back on top of the paralyzed Paulo, pulled his prey up to all fours with the palms of his strong hands on Paulo's belly and, crouching above him, thrust that long, thick curved cock back inside the young man and started pumping hard, his cock thickening and lengthening, filling Paulo once more and ever more possessively with Joy. And fucking him hard and roughly for all eternity.

Beat the Devil

The Dorfbewohner—the merchants, servants, sluggards, and patrons alike—of the ancient and wealthy mountain village of Uberusel in the Swabian Alps tripped oohing and ahhing and twittering out into the village square next to the city fountain overseen by the benign stone-cold figure of Prince Gerhard of the Swabian Hollenusterans. The snow on the cobblestones of the town gossip center that divided the patrician old upper town from the plebian lower town was melting, and the temperature had risen some twenty degrees in no longer than it took them to hear the clatter of horses' hooves at the gate of the lower village, where the road from the capital at Augsburg ended at the walled edge of the new town—deemed "new" because it was less than three hundred years old.

Summer had come early and swiftly to the village, it seemed, even if only a temporary anomaly, having brushed winter and spring aside in its rush to flood the village with smiles and laughter and coquettish looks between old and young villagers alike.

Such was the frivolity of the freakish change in the weather in the highest village of Swabia, set just below the rim of the bowl holding the gigantic shimmering Lake Nufenen, that they barely noticed the glossy black-painted carriage drawn by four massive black stallions that had drawn up beside the fountain. The ominously arresting steeds were clopping their hooves impatiently on the cobblestones and turning malevolent red-eyed glances to all sides, daring the cavorting Dorfbewohner to come near, and ready to fly off again up the steep and narrow passage to the gate of the count's castle, the Schloss perched oppressively near the highest ridge, hovering at a distance above its heavily taxed citizenry, and then, seemingly on up into the heavens.

The horses calmed and turned to stony salute, as if on command, as the carriage door opened, and out stepped a large-framed but goodly proportioned man elegantly dressed in black silk that shimmered in the suddenly hot sunlight and stretched to the limit over bulging muscles. His billowy cape swept almost down to the tops of his gleaming black leather boots. His countenance, albeit handsome in a rugged way, was also a disturbing combination of danger and connivance. His goatee was pointed, as were his ears, and when he opened his mouth to smile—or, rather, to grimace—his teeth gave the impression of a gnashing carnivore. He wore a black beaver-skin top hat, which was planted firmly on his head.

The horses quivered in unison and lowered their heads and looked away from the carriage as the heavy boots of the man hit the cobblestones with such force that the nearby villagers declared in years following that the earth shook—that they lost their joy at the unexpected warmth of the sun momentarily when struck with the sensation that an earthquake was beginning to build under their feet.

"I knew instantly that he was trouble," Dieter, the village barber, said to his customers in irritating repetition many season hence. "He had that look of an Aargauen about him. I told the sheriff as much at the time. But count's man that he was, the sheriff did nothing for us below the Schloss walls."

If Dieter had hinted as much either than or in the ensuing days—most certainly to the count's sheriff—none would have paid him heed, as Dieter was regarded then as now as more the village idiot than its barber. But if anyone reliable had made the suggestion then, what came about later might have been prevented. No, less than "might have," alas, as, truth be told, there

96

was no one below the count's walls who could have stood in the path of what Damien Handlanger wanted to do.

The charge of being an Aargauen, however, would have at least placed many in the village, who later learned to regret those short number of warm days, in awareness of possible danger.

The Swabians of Germany and the Swiss canton of Aargau had been in a stalemate war for nearly a century over the waters of Lake Nufenen, which occupied a basin plateau high in the alps on the German-Swiss border and fed mighty rivers running both south into Switzerland and north into the rich agricultural basin of the German princedoms.

Many had been the schemes of both sides to master the waters of the lake and to deny them to their neighbor. And Uberusel—under the tutelage of one of the most reclusive and reputedly cruel counts of all princedom—was the Swabian bastion protecting the headwaters of the great river running down into Germany from the lake.

Having reached the ground, and while two silent, grotesquely formed coachmen lowered two large trunks from atop the carriage down to the stones of the village center court, the black-clothed man turned and gave a languidly sweeping gaze around the Dorfbewohner who had poured out into the square to revel in the appearance of a summer sun in the last week of what had been an especially miserable winter. Those of the villagers who felt the power and piercing presence of his stare instinctively shrank from this obviously wealthy and powerful stranger and gave him a broad circle of space. Even the ground snow retreated from him, and the cobblestones hissed from the heat.

He turned and raised his hand to the open carriage door, and an angel appeared at the top step and stood there, smiling with apparent delight at the dancing and prancing of the invigorated villagers around the central fountain. He was a vision of beauty, dressed all in white vestments studded with transparent gemstones that sparkled in reflected light from the sun. Blond curls encircled his perfectly figured head like a halo, and he glowed in the morning sunlight. Although a young man, he had all of the innocent beauty of a boy. His body was perfectly formed, but he was willowy and small of stature.

And his smile lit up the square in heady competition with the unexpected summer sun in winter.

Now the villagers turned to the young man and danced and pranced around the carriage in preference to the fountain. All eyes were on him, and they pressed closer, into the circle of steaming cobblestones, eyes only for him, no longer captured by the feeling of malevolence radiating from his older companion in black.

The young man turned his eyes from those he had captured just by being there, as he stood at the top of the carriage steps, and toward his traveling companion, who was holding his hand up to the youth. The youth took the hand and descended the carriage steps. A sigh rolled through the convivial crowd in the square as his delicate, white-booted feet kissed the ground.

His eyes still riveted to the young man, a brave man separated from the encircling Dorfbewohner and stepped forward.

"Welcome to Uberusel, gracious travelers," he murmured, eyes only for the young man. "How may we be of service to you?"

"Who has the most presentable house in the village?" the black-suited man asked. His voice was unexpected. Yes, it had the air about it of "this is a command," but it was a rich, velvety baritone that was not only highly pleasant and soothing but also was arousing in ways men will know but not speak of and can hardly begin to define until it is too late for them to regain what they have lost.

The voice was of such authority that the villager turned to look directly into the eyes of the black-suited man, lost now to his authority and power and never to deny him anything from this point on.

"I must not prevaricate," the man said. "It is not a matter of vanity or pride that makes me say it, but the finest house here is mine. I am the Burgermeister—the mayor—of Uberusel. It is my house that is the most presentable."

"Then call your men to carry the trunks, and I and Camael will be your guests. My name is Damien Handlanger."

There was no discussion or negotiation of the matter. The Burgermeister accepted the self-proclaimed invitation without question and, calling forth, by name, a quartet of burly men from the swirl of the cavorting crowd, bid them to lift the trunks and carry them before the guests to the formidable timber and stuccoed mansion at the corner of the square and the main street leading up toward the count's Schloss.

"Hold a minute," Handlanger muttered, as the four men lifted the trunks with a huff and a groan and began to stagger through the crowd to the edge of the square. "Those four men. What would be their occupations?"

"Hans is a stonemason, and Gunther works with the dike system up at the lake, ensuring the proper flow of our river. The other two are just heavy lifters, construction workers, although Josef, the larger of the two, is gifted at engineering problems."

"Good," the man in black answered. "Have them come up to our rooms after dinner. And they are to bring wine."

"But these are not the men to be socializing with in this village," the Burgermeister answered in somewhat of a wounded huff. "They have never even been in my house. We are a wealthy town. There are many prominent families here. And some of them have lovely daughters." The last sentence was said in sotto voce, and the Burgermeister was flashing a lascivious wink at his newfound guest. "And several among those are very accommodating," the Burgermeister whispered.

"All in good time," Handlanger snapped, which brought the Burgermeister up short. The tone of his guest's voice sent shivers down his spine. Handlanger's voice modulated into silkiness once more. "Lest you misunderstand, I am an architect. These are strong-looking men, and you describe skills I may have need of. That is what I wish to see them about."

Chastened, the Burgermeister turned toward his home in embarrassment and began leading the two guests toward his front step, standing on which could be seen his buxom wife, the downstairs maid who brazenly held her position on the stoop because of her position in the Burgermeister's bed, and a teeming gaggle of gawking and bumptious children.

Once the three were beyond the steaming circle of stones, a whip was cracked, horses neighed and pawed the ground with the clang of metal horseshoes on stone, and the massive black carriage was thundering off and had disappeared from view almost before it had reached the enfolding arms of a narrow passageway headed into the upper village.

As the Burgermeister and his awesome guests processed, a lane opened for them, less because of the authority of the Burgermeister than for the shudder-inducing passage of the man in the black suit and his companion. They would have averted their eyes from him anyway, but the presence of the beautiful angel in white gave them something tangible to fawn upon as he passed and to dream about and, woman and man alike, to speculate about and to entertain arousing sensations over.

Not all in the square were so overcome in their senses—enticing, arousing, amused, and fearsome all at once—at the duo the black carriage had brought to the town square. Standing in the shadows, in the small copse of trees sheltering the city fountain, stood the count's sheriff, Maxmilian. Not a native of the village, but a former soldier from the north of Germany, Maxmilian was more worldly than any of these country bumpkins. He had been in the world, had seen both good and evil. And lately, in service to and in the bed of the count, he had learned much of domination and cruelty.

Sometimes Maxmilian himself had been good and sometimes he had been evil, and he was a keen judge of humankind. He watched the arrival of Damien Handlanger and his young protégé, Camael, with eyes that were open and calculating. And he knew that his work, as the count's sheriff, and as a protector of Swabia was being cut large for him. He wondered what reward was in store for him in the Schloss for a discerning report on the events in the village square that morning.

* * * *

Bringing order to the house of the Burgermeister should be his first priority, Damien thought, as he looked with disgust at the boisterous brats surrounding the Burgermeister's buxom and pinched-nosed wife as they approached Handlanger's new, if temporary, home. The wife first, certainly. No fool she, and a schemer and gossip to boot. The slut of a housemaid was less of a problem. She had the slouch of a dullard about her. The brats must be dispensed with immediately; Damien could do nothing useful with them swarming through the structure.

He was, however, presented with other avenues to start with first. It had been a boon to have identified helpers so soon. First them—and then the symbols of authority, perhaps.

As luck would have it, though, the village priest was the first one to work on. Not long after Damien and Camael had been shown to a commodious apartment of three rooms, on the first level above the street, with a chamber for each of them separated by a common room—where Damien planned to do common things after his dinner—the church bell started to ring and the Burgermeister attended them and said a required mass was soon to begin.

Damien was disgusted and his stomach churned at the mere thought of a mass, but he was new to the village and to his plan. This was the most delicate phase of the plan, its initiation, so there was nothing to be done but for him to signal to Camael and to follow the Burgermeister and his disruptive brood across the square to the main village church.

Priester Anasvindo was at the altar already, preparing the elements, as his premier congregants entered and took their place in the front pews. His eyes went immediately to the blond angel. He'd seen the arrival. He'd been drawn to the square along with the others because of the unannounced harbinger sun of summer and had stood at the edge of the teeming throng to watch the descent from the carriage of the curious, repelling, compelling strangers.

The malevolent force in black had made him tremble and lift his cross involuntarily to shake uncontrollably between him and the apparition. And then the angel had appeared at the door to the carriage, and Priester Anasvindo had been transported into his other world. The effect of this perfect young man was such on him that the priest had withdrawn from the edge of the crowd, a clawed hand pressed firmly into the yielding shoulder of a chorister who had been practicing in the church before they all felt the call of the sunshine, and he took the village youth into the sacristy and fucked all of the urges out of himself that the appearance of the white angel had aroused.

And now he, the compelling angel, was here, in his church sanctuary, sitting in the first of the pews, and, as the ritual began, was singing in a clear, pure soprano that floated out above all of the rest. The chorister who had felt Priester Anasvindo's rod was missing, snuffling and sniffing in the bell tower, but the young stranger's voice was even more beautiful than his.

Priester Anasvindo turned, not really knowing why he was doing so, and beckoned to the young singer of beauty, inviting him to take the place of the missing chorister in the pews behind the altar.

And to his surprise, after looking to the man in black for guidance, the white angel had glided up into the choir pew and lifted his voice once more over all of the rest in an Ava Maria.

Priester Ansavindo turned the ritual over to two monks assisting him and moved back to his throne chair next to the choir pews, closed his eyes and smiled, and let the angelic music wash over him.

Damien Handlanger knew the instant when the setting had changed inside the church. Damien saw all; indeed, Damien planned and maneuvered most of what would happen in the village of Uberusel over the coming days.

He gave the natural unveiling of his greater scheme time enough to become established and then he rose from his pew, slipped out at the side, and crept through the door into the sacristy. His timing had been perfect, as he knew it would be. He had timed it all from the moment he looked up beyond the altar and saw the priest's throne empty and the new chorister's position vacant.

Camael, naked and marble skinned, was laying on his back on the table where the elements were prepared. His legs were spread wide, his toes daintily pointed, a beatific smile on his face. And the old Priester Ansavindo, his Cossack drawn up around his waist, was bent over Camael's perfectly formed lithe torso, moving his pelvis between those daintily drawn-out legs, and babbling in Latin over his good fortune at dipping his surprisingly hard stick in the young angel's sweet honeypot. Camael was not resisting in any way; indeed, he was moving his hips in rhythm with the priest's, digging his finely manicured fingers into the old man's shoulders, and urging him on with talk of what a melting man he was—how much Camael melted at having him moving inside him.

Without a sound, Damien untied his cod piece and let the flap fall and his monstrous tool flop out. Three shakes and he was prepared for anointing. He slipped in behind the priest, grabbed the old bugger with a tight grip of both hands at his neck, reared back his hips and spiked the priest's asshole in one long tearing plunge that lifted the old man off Camael.

The two older men reeled around the room in a macabre dance, the priest totally unable to shake off his assaulter and invader, as Damien's superhuman cock had the priest fully and deeply skewered. Priester Ansavindo gurgled in choking tones, the fingers on his neck sizzling with branding heat, and danced, feet off the ground, as the taller, stronger man forced his cock up into the priest's intestines and began filling him with possessing venom until the priest felt it burble in the back of his throat. Finished, Damien pushed the old man off his cock in a gesture of disgust, and the priest fell in a moaning heap at his feet.

As this transpired, Camael sat up on the edge of the table and smiled his beatific smile down on the priest that said all was right with the world.

After he'd taken his hands away from the priest's neck and let his body sink to the floor, Damien towered over his prey. He saw, with satisfaction, the branding marks of his fingers on the priest's neck and knew that the priest was his now. To prove it, with Priester Ansavindo now clutching at his boots, Damien gave him a cruel kick and turned to Camael and said, "Dress. We depart now."

"No," the priest moaned. "No. Do not leave me. I must have your cock again."

Damien obliged him, just to be sure. Control of the priest was important. As the priest moaned in combined fear and wanting, Camael jumped down of the table and started clothing himself. Damien lifted the priest from the floor and forced him belly down on the table top and, his four heavy-hanging balls quickly rejuvenating, entered him once more, strongly and deeply. He pumped the priest at greater length now, giving him two gasping ejaculations before Damien filled him once again with the venom that would make him forget all but what Damien wanted him to remember—ensuring that whatever Damien wanted, the priest wanted for him as well.

"Perhaps it was good to start there," Damien said to Camael as they prepared to return to the church service in what seemed to be an eternity of life-changing fucking for the now-branded priest but was bare moments for those taking mass out in the sanctuary. "These villagers are such a tediously gullible lot. The church is a major institution here. For my plan to succeed, I must not only neutralize but also master the church here."

Back in the Burgermeister's house, dinner completed, and the four burly workman summoned to Damien's rooms and half insensitive with liquor, Damien gave each, in turn, a few never-to-be-forgotten blissful moments dipping in Camael's sweet honeypot in the young angel's chamber, and an eternity of total, splitting, stomach-reaching possession by Damien's manhood as they nearly choked on Damien's neck branding and were enlisted into his service by the calming venom of his deeply planted seed. By the end of the evening, Handlanger had enlisted the four mainstays of his plans for the people of Swabia.

The next day there only remained the task of bringing peace to the bustling and raucous household of the Burgermeister.

After dinner, Damien invited the Burgermeister up to their rooms for a game of draughts while smoking their pipes and drinking off their after-dinner flagons. As they played and talked and laughed and the Burgermeister disappeared increasingly into his cup, Camael rose from his chair and stumbled slightly as he passed the Burgermeister's chair and fell deftly into the village mayor's lap. The Burgermeister had been losing game after game anyway through inattention, as he could not keep his eyes off the white angel and found that he had difficulty keeping his hands off the youth as well.

Once Camael was in his lap, accident or otherwise, all was lost. They were kissing almost before the Burgermeister realized what was happening. And his hands were moving over the youth and undoing this and that and moving in this fold and finding that flesh. And his own codpiece was open by some unknown hand, and his erect cock was luxuriating in the warmth and closeness of a sweet, tight channel, as Camael descended into his lap and then raised himself and lowered himself and continued to do so, their lips locked together. The Burgermeister flowed and groaned and moaned in paradise.

But then he was descending straight to hell, as he was roughly drawn from the youth, stripped of his leggings, and split asunder by a killing pole, invading and filling and expanding and digging inside him. He opened his mouth to scream, only to have the air choked out of him by strong, hot pokers at his neck. Choking him, making his eyeballs pop, searing his flesh. He screamed within, getting a vivid glimpse of the fires of hell. He was almost swept away by the horror of it, when he felt the beginning of the flow deep inside him. He subsided into a calm that he had never experienced before. He sighed in full sexual satisfaction, steeped also in a feeling of want that he had never felt before. Not a want of the young white angel, Camael, but incomprehensibly of the other one, the powerful and foreboding Damien Handlanger. The man in black who had his oak of a cock so far up inside him that the Burgermeister felt it would pop out of his mouth. And although he'd never lain with a man before, he knew that he'd never been as satisfied and filled before as he was now. And he did not want to lose that sensation.

He looked up, panting at the monster of a man who now stood over him, looking down at him, possessing him as much with his eyes and mere demeanor as he had done with his cock. Still dressed in black, his codpiece flapped open, freeing the longest, thickest, blackest cock the Burgermeister had ever seen on a man, below which hung four heavy, globular balls the king bull of the pastures would be proud of.

The man spoke. "You may have Camael for the night. But in the morning, you will clear the house of everyone but the male servants, who you will bring to me one by one. And then you will identify the best butcher and provisioner in the village and bring them to me as well. Then you shall dine like a king and I shall bed you like a bull for as long as it pleases me."

"Yes, master," the Burgermeister murmured. "But why? Why Camael? Why cannot it be you tonight?"

Damien's mouth curled up in a cruel, satisfied smile. This had been somewhat of a test, and the Burgermeister had shown that he was enslaved.

"Let me show you all and then I will ask you again. But choose carefully. It will be for all eternity."

The Burgermeister lay huddled there, awestroke, staring up at Damien, as the monster of a man stripped off his black, silken clothing and stood there naked before the village mayor, bulging with muscle, smiling malevolently, nubs of horns where his cap had fallen away. He stood there on heavily pelted goat legs and cloven feet, his eyes searching those of the Burgermeister's for signs of rejection or indecision. Facing the village mayor with the totality of what was transpiring.

Seeing no sign of rejection or indecision, without asking the question, Damien lifted the Burgermeister as if he were some downy cushion and carried him into his chamber, tossed him on the pallet, and fucked him into hell in waves and waves of takings, the exhausted and nearly spent village mayor always wanting more, always on the point of expiring, but never taken farther—as Damien wanted the house cleared of those gossipy women and bratty children and also knew that the man he was taking into hell was necessary for his plan.

Camael sat in the middle chamber for a short time, smiling his beatific smile. Temptation—an invitation to succumbing to basic instincts—was no longer needed with the Burgermeister. At length, Camael rose and moved into his chamber and slept alone. He was far beyond surprise. Time and time again he had slept alone because of the choices men were prone to make.

* * * *

The men of Uberusel were so susceptible to the choice that Damien Handlanger offered that it was mere days before Damien could put his plan into action, in a house cleared of women and overflowing with Burgermeister, priest, servants, workman, and tradesmen, all yearning for Handlanger's cock and the venom of his four hefty balls, all marked with the brands of his fingers on their necks, and all satisfied just enough by Handlanger to want more and more.

By day the men planned and gathered equipment and supplies and made up schedules. And by night, Handlanger had them all writhing on the floor as he moved from man to man, fucking them totally and filling them with his calming hell-paradise venom. Camael, in turn, sat above the fray, smiling his dazzling smile, present as a hint of a choice of another road. Nearly all of the chosen men of Uberusel, however, were far beyond the temptation of Camael that had brought them, one by one to their master.

Only the priest began to backslide, gifted as he was in second chances on demand and shifting "truth" with a never-ending litany of legalistic "how many angels can dance on the head of a pin?" garble. But Damien still needed the church to remain silent in the face of what was happening in the village, and he knew that every church and churchman had his price. Seeing the priest's gaze shift away from him and back to Camael, Damien was quick to discern that the appetites of the man, like those of the institution, were broad and insatiable. Damien took Camael aside then and instructed him on what he was to do on "the day."

Damien was greatly pleased with himself that his plan had never made him mount the steep and narrow roadway up to the Schloss. Handlanger had actually been apprehensive about the need to enlist the count, and apprehension was not an emotion that Handlanger was accustomed to feel.

But actually the count was something else altogether. The count was more an adversary than prey. Damien sensed that there were deeper hells than his and stronger, crueler devils. The very vibrations that came off the Schloss on the mountaintop gave Handlanger pause. Something inside him told him that the count was an evil force of an older, more powerful order than he was.

And there was another force that Damien hadn't counted on and that now, just one night before the plan was to go into operation, stood, unexpectedly in his path.

It was with trembling hands and legs that the Burgermeister knocked on Damien's door and informed him that there was a visitor without who insisted on speaking with him.

Damien was irritated, as he wanted to rest before the night's all-important work. But he knew that the visit must be an important one, or the Burgermeister would have just turned the visitor away.

"Good evening, sir," the sheriff of Uberusel said with a strong voice of authority as he entered the room. Two hard-bodied guardsmen entered behind him and stood, hands on swords on either side of the door. Camael rose from the table and moved into the shadows of the room. "I have come because of some strange happenings in the village. Some events that all trace back to you. Events that have occurred since your arrival. And I must call you to account to explain yourself to me, in the name of the count whose castle protects this village."

Handlanger picked up a sharp knife and an apple from a basket on the table in front of him and slowly began to peel it, taking his time, as he viewed the sheriff under droopy lids. The sheriff was handsome and manly, an excellent specimen. Damien lamented that he so rarely enjoyed his work. But he knew he'd enjoy the sheriff immensely. There was something about him. He was not like other men. Other men did not inflame Damien's loins as this comely warrior standing before him did.

"I must answer to you, must I?" he said at length. "I think not."

"If not here, then at the goal," the sheriff said gruffly. "If you will not cooperate, my men will . . ."

"What men would that be?" Damien answered in a self-satisfied voice.

The sheriff whipped his body around to find the doorway behind him empty.

"What? Where?"

"Perhaps you should check through that doorway over there," Damien answered as he motioned nonchalantly with the hand holding the knife.

The sheriff turned and strode to the door indicated and threw it open.

Then he stood there, mouth agape.

Camael was servicing both of the guards; all three were naked, the metal swords of the guardsmen well out of reach, their flesh swords hard at conquest. One guard was sitting on the side of the bed, Camael astride his lap, moving his channel on the soldier's cock. The soldier was moaning deeply, lost to the world. The second guardsmen was crouched over the thighs of the other two, and also was fully sheathed in Camael's channel. It was clear that the two were in no condition to guard anything as their cocks made mutual love to the white angel.

The sheriff made to move to the bed, but Damien suddenly was standing behind him, holding him in place in strong arms and his knife blade at the sheriff's throat.

"Watch," Damien muttered gruffly. "Watch until they are done. And then tell me what you want to do." Damien found he was breathing heavily, much affected by the closeness of the sheriff, by the hardness and suppleness of him. His scent, the feel of his silken hair upon Damien's cheek as he held the sheriff's head back against his, the knife at the younger man's throat.

The three fucked on. The Burgermeister and the others of the household entered the room and spread out around the edges and all watched intently, as Camael gave the two guards the fuck of their lives.

Feeling the sheriff trembling within his grasp and reaching around his waist and feeling what he knew he'd feel—an engorged cock straining at its codpiece—Damien gave a signal to Camael and Camael brought the two guards to ejaculation. At another signal, strong arms of the henchmen around the periphery reached out and pulled away the guards and manhandled them out of the room, never to be seen again.

"Now what do you want?" Damien whispered in the sheriff's ear.

"I want him," the sheriff moaned.

Camael turned and sat on the bed and leaned back on his elbows and opened his marble-white legs wide. He turned up his hips, showing a rosy redbud of a hole that belied him having just ridden two cocks together.

"So, take him," Damien murmured.

He released the sheriff, who went at Camael with the guttural growl of a forest animal. Camael smiled his beatific smile and opened his lips to the sheriff's tongue and his channel to the sheriff's throbbing cock. They fucked for an eternity, with the sheriff attacking in a frenzy and Camael draining him again and again and again in a myriad of positions—until the sheriff was exhausted and collapsed on top of the white angel.

Damien watched the ritual with sensations rising in his body that he rarely felt and never acknowledged. Tantalizing arousal, unexpected jealousy, the panting of want. He wanted the sheriff. That was an unknown quantity for him—as was the jealousy of seeing Camael pleasuring the sheriff as he so fully did. It was only then, when the sheriff was fully satiated and at the nadir of his strength and will, that Damien strode over to the two, releasing his codpiece with one hand and grabbing the sheriff by his hair and pulling him off Camael with the other.

"This is almost too easy," he muttered, as he encircled the sheriff's throat with his searing fingers and thrust up into his channel with his invading cock. But as the sheriff's channel grasped Damien's cock and drew it deep inside, the muscles of the walls were making Damien moan in ecstasy at the love being made to his cock, and Damien loosened his hold on the sheriff's throat. The only searing branding being done in this coupling would be on what passed for Handlanger's heart.

* * * *

The next night, Priester Anasvindo was alone, communing deeply with great sighs, with Camael in the otherwise empty Burgermeister's house, while Damien and his converts were on the cliffs overlooking the mouth of the river flowing from Lake Nufenen down into Swabia past Uberusel. The priest, as Damien had surmised, had attempted to slip out of the Burgermeister's house in the flurry of preparations, with the Schloss hovering over the village being his certain goal. But, as arranged, Camael was there, at the door, smiling his beatific smile, running his beautiful hands over his hips, the invitation obvious.

"What could a short dip hurt?" the priest thought as Camael led him off into a side chamber. It was nothing for Camael to entrap the foolish and easily beguiled old priest's cock into a paradise that went on in waves and waves of taking and moaning until the earth shook in a way that did not match the movement of the earth brought on by the multiple ejaculations the white angel had been coaxing out of the old man's testes.

The villagers of Uberusel were awakened by the earth moving and the sound of the overshadowing mountain caving in. They ran out into the cobblestoned square of Uberusel and milled around, lamenting that the world was coming to an end. And in a way that was what had been in the devilish plan. Handlanger had assembled just the right mix of skills in his conquests to cause boulders to rain into the outlet of water down into Swabia from the lake and to irrevocably close up that entrance for all time. Henceforth none of the water would reach the fields in the lowlands of Swabia via this channel, but would, instead, be bringing even more lush plantings to the Swiss plateau in the canton of Aargau.

The sheriff was not on the cliffs over the lake. His assignment was to guard the gates of the count's Schloss, ensuring that the count did not get wind of what was happening and possibly bring even more power to bear than Damien Handlanger had. Then he was to join Damien and Camael on the Swiss side of the lake and go with them down into the Aargauen canton and into the bed of Damien, who had not been able to shake his moaning for the undulation of the sheriff's channel walls on his cock.

The sheriff smiled to himself as he heard the rumbling of the mountain that would dry up the river channel down into Swabia. He would not be here for the anticipated resulting death-bringing drought. He would be expected to be wherever Damien would be. They had fucked through the previous night, and the sheriff could tell from the moans of Damien as he was taken again and again, the sheriff using the highly skilled channel muscles on Damien's digging cock as he had been taught in his long nights in the Schloss with the count, that he had as much power over the devil as the devil had over him.

Inside the Schloss, the count heard the earth move and groan even as the villagers had, and he smiled and shrugged off his brocade robes and waited for the door of his chamber to open. And when it did, the sheriff entered and disrobed, lay back on the count's heavily cushioned bed, and spread his legs for his lord and master. As he mastered his servant once more, almost loath to lose him for any time in the service of Damien Handlanger but unable to forego the ecstasy of having a spy in the devil's bed, the count counted the hours before he could safely bring a miracle to the village and the valleys of Swabia by opening the sluice gates of the secret underground spillways running from the bed of Lake Nufenen, under the foundations of the Schloss, and into the now-drying riverbed running through the village of Uberusel.

111

Shark

"Pretty hot work."

"You can say that again, sir. And that's a pretty hot car you got there."

"Thanks. I'm addicted to Corvettes."

"What year?"

"This year. I usually trade up every other year."

"Shit, man. That's beyond my imagination. Oh, sorry for the 'shit.' We were told not to curse around the motorists."

"No problem. It's a fuckin' good set of wheels."

"Yes, it fuckin' is." The young flagman flashed a broad smile, made comfortable by the man's congeniality, and moved a couple of steps closer in toward the windshield of the metallic blue Corvette convertible. He was minimally dressed, in keeping with the high heat of summer in western Kansas. He had the requisite fluorescent green safety vest, but no shirt, showing a set of very serious biceps, a tattoo of a sunburst on one. He was blond, with a long ponytail trailing out of the back of his safety helmet, but he'd been tanned deeply by the realities of his job. "Saw the license plate. Shark. That your name or something?"

"No, you could say more that that's what I do," the dark-haired—with gray streaks—dusky-complexioned, goateed middle-aged man behind the Corvette's wheel said, with a laugh. "Hard job standing out here changing a sign from 'slow' to 'stop' hour on end."

"Yeah, gets pretty hot and dry out here—and monotonous, 'cept when someone tools up in a flash car like this one. We've been working this stretch of highway 50 ten miles short of Cimarron for nearly a year now—with nearly a year to go. Pretty much unforgivable desert out here. But it's a job. Don't know what I'll do when the road's done."

"I've got some beer on ice in the chest behind my seat. Could I entice you with one?"

"No, sorry, sir. Can't drink on the job. Sounds wonderful, though."

"I've got bottled water too—ice cold. You allowed to accept that?"

"Yes, thanks, sir."

"Don't need to call me that," the man said as he reached into the cooler and came up with a bottle of designer water. "You can call me Beel, if you've got a name to exchange."

The young man smiled as he reached over and accepted the water. "Zeke. They call me Zeke. Thanks for the water, Bill. I'm sorry you got stuck in line just at the changeover. It shouldn't be more than a couple of more minutes. You might want to put the top up on the Vette, though. It's really hot out here."

"I'm used to heat, Zeke. And it's Beel, not Bill. It's short for something—but I'm sure you don't want to get into that now. It's Friday. You got to do this on Saturday and Sunday too?"

"Naw, we've got the weekend off. And today's payday. We'll be hitting Wyatt's hard."

"Wyatt's?"

"The local pool and poker hall in Cimarron. We cool off in there Friday nights—trying to double our pay and slaking our thirst from a week of dust out here on the unfinished road."

"So, you're a local, Zeke?"

"Yeah. Cimarron born and raised—which isn't half as exciting as it might sound. This town's heyday was back in the Wild West days. Nothin' exciting has happened here in decades."

"Maybe someone should change that," the Corvette driver said, with a smile. "Any good motels in Cimarron?"

114

"Well, there's the Cimarron Hotel and the Blue Jay Inn. But notice I didn't answer the 'any good?' question."

"One more private than the other one?"

"Guess that would be the Blue Jay Inn. Here comes the pilot car now, so I gotta step back in the slot and you'll be on your way in no time now. Thanks for the water . . . Beel."

"And thanks for the conversation and view, Zeke. Maybe I'll see you around."

"Yeah, maybe so," Zeke answered. He returned to his position, ready to turn his sign from 'stop' to 'slow' without another thought to the man in the Corvette—although he watched the tail of the car drive off with appreciation and envy.

* * * *

"So, you allowed to accept that beer now?"

"What? Oh, the man with the Vette. Bill, was it?"

"No, it's Beel. And I'd really like to buy you that beer— for leading me to Wyatt's. This does look like it's where it's happening."

"Not that anything's happening much around here," Zeke said with a snort.

"I think we'll manage," Beel said in a quiet voice, a little knowing smile on his face.

Out of the automobile, the man—Beel—looked more commanding to Zeke than how he'd remembered him when looking down into the driver's seat of the convertible. He was tall and barrel-chested. Looked like he worked out still, even at his age—which also didn't look as old as before when the gray streaks in his hair and goatee were more prominent. He was wearing an expensive-looking gray tweed Western-cut jacket, matching well-pressed trousers, and finely tooled leather cowboy boots—which gave him the look of a wealthy Texas oilman or cattle rancher. As far as Zeke could tell, with a thought to the Corvette the man had been driving earlier, that was probably what he was.

For his part, Zeke cleaned up real good too—after he'd showered off the dust of the road construction out on route 50 and shampooed his hair, which now showed its golden highlights. He was wearing faded, but clean, tight blue jeans and a tight red

T-shirt, exhibiting bulging thighs and a chest tapering down to a flat belly and small waist. All together the package showed that working road construction earned muscles honestly.

"You play poker or pool?" Zeke asked after he accepted the beer.

"You could say that—both. You think you could get me into a poker game with your construction buddies?"

Zeke could, but he began to regret doing so more and more as the evening wore on. His buddies were losing badly. He was losing too—but then managed to recoup most of what he was losing. So, unlike his increasingly glowering buddies, who watched their week's pay slide across the table to sit in front of the quiet, smiling, dark stranger with the strange name, Zeke almost didn't notice that his pile was beginning to diminish too.

"You play pool?" Beel asked Zeke, as the poker players began drifting away, unhappy and pockets nearly empty.

"Yeah. I'm said to be pretty good at it," Zeke answered, eyeing Beel's newly won stack of bills. Zeke, in fact, knew he was better than "pretty good" at it, and he figured on getting what he'd lost and some of what his construction friends had donated as well.

He wasn't as good as Beel was, and it soon became apparent that Beel could show him a thing or two about holding the stick and picking his shots. As Zeke's weekly pay slowly moved from his pocket to Beel's, Beel started showing signs of taking pity on him. From time to time he'd stop Zeke as he was ready to make a shot and stand close behind him, showing him how to hold the cue and line up shots. When he did this, Zeke felt an electric current flow through him, but he was concentrating more on his depleting funds and, after the first demonstration, he could see that what Beel was showing him was helpful and was stemming his losses—sort of.

But there came a time when Zeke had lost far more than he could afford to do. He begged off another break of the balls and moved toward the table where the poker players who had been fleeced were drowning their sorrows in beer and commiserating over their loses, but the glares they all gave him showed that it would be at least a couple of hours before they would forgive him for bringing that card shark into their midst.

He veered off and collapsed into a chair at another table. He didn't see Beel sit down beside him, but he felt that electric current course through his body when Beel put a reassuring hand on his shoulder.

Beel leaned into him and said. "I bet taking a ride in my Vette will help you feel a little bit better. And maybe there's something I can help you with in getting some of your money back."

"A ride in your Corvette?" Zeke asked through a snuffle. He'd wanted to cry, but there was no way that he was going to let any of the construction workers—or Beel—see him do that. "Shit man, I've never ridden in a Vette."

"Now's your chance. It needs letting the lead out of its engine. With all that construction on 50, it was stop and go all afternoon. You can maybe show me where there's some straightaway at night where I can let it blow its engine clean and we'll have a ball."

They sped out on a dirt road north from Cimarron into desolate ranch land, eventually running out of road at the entrance of a homestead marked by log poles with a log cross bar making an arch over the road into a square bordered by a small group of deteriorating buildings with no lights showing.

"What's in there?" Beel asked.

"It's the old Anderson place. They're all dead and gone now, and no one's been able to track down any heirs yet—not that there's anything in there worth handing over."

Beel turned the Vette and drove in under the crossbar and into the courtyard all of the buildings faced. Then he turned off the motor and turned to Zeke. "I told you that maybe there was a way you could get some of that money back."

"Yeah, how's that?" Zeke asked. "I'm not offing your wife or anything." He laughed nervously.

"I don't have a wife, Zeke. I like men."

That took a moment to sink in, but then Zeke shrank as close to the passenger door of the tight-fitting Corvette as he could. "Hey, man. I'm not into any of that shit."

"Then you don't know what you're missing, do you?" Beel asked. "It's not a hard way to earn cash. Certainly not as hard as standing out on a dusty road turning a sign around every half hour."

"I ain't done nothin' like that, man. There's some things money don't buy."

"Oh, well, I guess we'll go back to town then," Beel said, as he turned the ignition key and the Corvette revved up in a rumble. "I've got a roof over my head tonight. How much longer can you cover that department?"

"Wait, man, let me think," Zeke said, the panic in his voice palpable.

"Sure, you think about it," Beel said, as he switched the engine off. His hand moved from the key to Zeke's thigh, and Zeke groaned at the electric touch of him, feeling himself harden up at the mere thought of what was being proposed—and the touch of Beel's long, electric fingers on his thigh. It wasn't as if Zeke hadn't thought about doing it before.

"What sort of money are we talking about?"

"I jack you off and you get fifty back. Seventy-five if you blow me. Two hundred back for each fuck."

"Each? Oh, shit, man." There was a moment of silence then, as Zeke fought off hyperventilation—and watched in horror and fascination as Beel moved his hand to Zeke's basket. Zeke knew Beel could feel him hard—and he knew that weakened any denial or negotiating position he had. He needed some of that money back. He also was aroused; he couldn't kid himself about that. He certainly understood that Beel's hand on his cock understood he was aroused. "I'd fuck you?"

"No, that's not the way it would work, Zeke. I'd fuck you."

"Oh, man. I . . . don't know."

"I like you. I want you, Zeke. So, I'll tell you what. I'll double the offer." Beel was speaking with confidence, and this was being driven home, because he already was pulling Zeke's zipper down. And Zeke wasn't stopping him.

All Zeke could manage was a weak-voiced whimper, "I won't do any blowjob."

"We'll manage," Beel said. And then he laughed, a deep-throated laugh, as he pulled Zeke's nearly hard cock out of his opened fly. He didn't take it in hand right away. He stopped long enough to pull Zeke's T-shirt over his head. Then he turned toward the young blond in the seat and, with one hand, grabbed Zeke's ponytail at the base, and pulled his head back tight with the headrest. His other hand took Zeke's cock and began to stroke.

Zeke groaned at the electric touch of Beel's hand on his cock. He gave a little yip when Beel leaned over and took a nipple in his teeth. He moaned as Beel's mouth moved up to the hollow of his neck and sucked him hard there. All of the time, the motion on Zeke's cock was progressively becoming more rapid. Zeke turned his face toward Beel's and opened his mouth to him as Beel moved his lips up Zeke's cheek.

Then Zeke was gasping and writhing and bouncing his hips off the bucket seat of the Corvette, and his cock was being pumped with inhuman strength and pistoning motion.

Beel's tongue and lips freed Zeke's mouth and almost immediately the young man was crying out in surprise and ecstasy, as Beel's mouth sheathed his cock and a hand moved to Zeke's balls, squeezing and rolling them hard and pulling them away from his body. The vibration and suction of Beel's mouth was driving Zeke crazy—but only for seconds.

It was all over in a few brief moments, leaving Zeke exhausted and slack jawed.

"I have you now," Beel muttered, with a half laugh. "Step out of the car, Zeke."

"I . . . I don't think I can."

"Now, Zeke. It's time to earn back big money."

Zeke had never imagined it could be like this. The initial invasion of his virgin ass was a few seconds of excruciating pain, but after that no sensation of pain could have made Zeke forego the experience of Beel's cock working inside him.

Zeke was bent over the hood of the Corvette, his cheek to the warm metal, and Beel was palming his belly, pulling Zeke's midsection off the car surface and into Beel's pelvis with one hand and arching his back with a fist at the root of his ponytail, as Beel's cock filled and drilled him, sending flashes of electricity through Zeke's body. Beel's cock was vibrating and pulsing and forcing itself deep, deep inside Zeke's channel, stretching him, sending the mind-blowing pleasure of it through his body. Zeke's legs were jelly, but Beel was holding him up and pulling him higher, onto his toes and then letting him down on his heels with the strength of his buried and pumping cock.

It went on for more than an hour, and Zeke came twice more, before Beel gave a deep-throated, lusty laugh and flooded Zeke's insides with four strong, separate spoutings of ejaculate, which gave Zeke hot flashes that raced out to the ends of his extremities.

When Beel pulled out of him and released his belly and ponytail, Zeke slid to the earth beside the wheel of the Corvette.

Beel sat on the hood of the Corvette and looked down at Zeke. Zeke looked up at him and saw that Beel was still in monstrous erection.

"Again," Zeke murmured. It came out as a prayerful request.

"I think not," Beel answered. "It was nice, but I'm not sure it was worth $400."

"No, no. Again, please. I never knew . . . again, please. Not for money."

Beel laughed and stood down from the Corvette hood where he'd been perched. He leaned down and pulled Zeke up and lowered the young blond's back on the Corvette hood, spread his legs with fists encasing ankles, and thrust inside him strongly. Zeke cried out in surprise and shock and his eyes rolled up in his head, but he immediately started moaning and panting and working his hips in the ever-faster rhythm of the fuck that Beel was establishing and extending for endless time.

"I don't want to sleep alone," Beel said as they were cruising back into Cimarron. "I presume that even in a town this size you know of some presentable young man who will keep me warm tonight for a hundred bucks."

"I'll do it," Zeke shot back without hesitation. "Please."

Beel laughed. "I've had you already. I want variety."

"For free. I'll do it for free," Zeke whined.

But Beel ignored that and continued speaking. "An Hispanic maybe. Small and not too stale. But willing. You get me one and I'll sweeten your take by $200."

* * * *

120

His name was Manuel. Barely legal, and just starting doing it for money. He was small boned, and a bit delicate—and maybe just a little more swishy than Beel would have liked if he'd had a lineup to pick from. And when he saw Beel's cock, he cried out and headed for the door in the Blue Jay Inn motel. But Beel was too fast for him and covered his mouth with one hand as he pulled the frightened Hispanic down into his lap and proved that the Hispanic could—with considerable effort and grunting—take all of him, although it was seemingly magic that was required to get all of Beel inside him and the small Hispanic was gasping and working his mouth in a wide-gaped yawn as if he expected the head of the cock to appear on top of his tongue.

As Manuel felt the searching vibration and pulsing and electric current over his channel walls, he began to moan and melt into the lap fuck. Somehow Beel maneuvered his torso around so that his mouth sheathed Manuel's own cock, and they were working in consort as one pleasure-producing machine, as, like with Zeke, Manuel blew and rebuilt and blew again before Beel bathed his insides with ejaculate.

After that Manuel couldn't get enough of Beel throughout the night—and Beel demonstrated that there was no limit to what he had to give.

It was nearly dawn before they both slept. And it wasn't more than an hour later before the telephone in the room rang—on the side of the bed Manuel was facing, on his side, Beel's still-half-hard cock deep inside his channel.

Manuel picked up the receiver.

"It's Zeke Candrell," Manuel said sleepily. Then he went back to the telephone and what Zeke had to tell him put him on immediate alert. "He says the construction workers you took all of the money from last night are on their way here. They beat out of Zeke where you were. They've decided you cheated them, and they want their money back."

"Time to move on, then," Beel said in an almost jovial tone as he pulled out of the Hispanic youth and sat on the side of the bed and reached for his elegantly stenciled boots.

"Zeke says he'll meet you out at the edge of town. He wants to go with you."

"Tell him that's impossible. I ride alone—and I have his soul now, what further need do I have of his body."

Manuel disappeared as Beel was finishing dressing—but he reappeared in the passenger seat of the Corvette the older man had parked around on the side of the motel, shielded from view from the street, when Beel came out of the motel room.

Beel laughed and picked him up and carried him back into the motel room. He threw him in the motel room's closet and pulled the bed in front of the closet door—which is where the construction workers found Manuel five minutes later when they arrived at the motel room, its door gaping open.

Three hours later, west of Dodge City, on route 50, young, golden-blond, honestly muscled Jim Steele was standing at his family's mail box at the end of a long dusty dirt road back to the house and outbuildings of their cattle spread. He was on edge and a little piqued because he'd walked all this way down from the barn, where, stripped down to his jeans, he'd been putting the feed out for the horses, only to find there was no mail in the box.

The previous night hadn't been good for him. His steady, Gail, had let him feel her up, but she'd stopped his hand as his trembling finger was about to enter the wet darkness of her. He'd been keyed up and ready to blow ever since. He was feeling sorry for himself and wondering if he'd get anything before he turned old and gray.

He looked north, east, and west, away from the farm, at the slightly rolling, wholly monotonous countryside, wishing he were anywhere but here.

He heard the car approach just as he was walking back to the farm and then turned and looked back at the road when it didn't pass. He rubbed his eyes in disbelief and walked closer. What was a gorgeous new metallic-blue top-down Corvette convertible doing out here on route 50 between nowhere and nowhere else at 7:00 a.m. in the morning?

The driver, the lone passenger in the car, a dusky-complexioned man with an interesting, almost Asian face and black, gray-streaked hair and an unusual goatee smiled at him. Jim smiled back, hospitality being a hallmark of good, honest rancher farmers in the Kansas badlands.

"Hey, you sure look like you're in the need of a cooling drink," the stranger said. "Can I offer you a cold beer? Got them back here just in the cooler?"

"Too early for a beer, mister. But . . . thanks anyway."

"How about water then, you look like you've been standing out here forever waiting for something to happen."

"I feel like it . . . thanks for the water." Beel had already had the bottle out of the cooler and was holding it out toward Jim, across the seats of the Corvette. Out of politeness, Jim accepted it, which brought him to the side of the car. Just putting a hand on the passenger window well sent shudders of pleasure up Jim's spine. Nobody around here owned anything like this.

"There's nothin' gonna happen around here, I'm afraid. But standin' and lookin' at the horizon is a common activity in Kansas. Shit, this is a beautiful piece of equipment—uh, sorry for the cuss word."

"No problem. Yes, it's a fuckin' beautiful piece of heaven. You got a name?"

"Uh, yes, Jim. Jim Steele," Jim answered with a warm smile, disarmed by the stranger's comfort with cussing. "And you?" It was all natural pleasantries, the exchange of names being a long-practiced customs of friendliness and willingness to trust in the ranching and farming environment where everyone helps everyone else.

"I'm called Beel."

"Glad to meet cha', Bill."

"No, it's Beel. It's short for a much more complicated name, but we needn't go into that now. Say, if you're just at loose ends now and wishing there was some excitement in your life, how would you like to take a ride in a new Corvette?"

"Oh, man, would I ever!"

"Hop in. And you sure it's not too early for a beer or two."

"Well, if you twist my arm," Jim said happily as he opened the door to the Corvette and folded his hunky bulk into the passenger seat.

"It may come to that," Beel muttered under his breath, too quietly for Jim to hear, as he looked both east and west down the deserted route 50, pulled the Corvette back onto the road, and turned around, headed for the deserted Anderson spread.

Demon Spiral

"Go on, take them all. I know you want them."

Damon Wentworth was standing there with that skimpy bathing suit plastered to his groin, showing which side he dressed on, and had the platter of crab Rangoon pastries shoved up under Chris' chin. It hadn't been the crab Rangoon that Chris had had his eyes on as Wentworth came at him on the terrace in back of the fast-food restaurant chain owner's McMansion. The terrace was all a jumble with those—both new employees and some senior ones—invited to the Wentworth's pool party.

Chris was one of the new employees. He knew why he'd been invited to the party. He even knew why he'd been hired as an assistant manager of one of Wentworth's fast-food restaurants. He had been game for it and he'd been had by Wentworth before coming to this pool party. Wentworth was just his type: self-assured, an air of entitlement, twenty years older than he was but in expensive gym trim, a devilish look in his eyes, and curly black hair swirling on his chest and belly, arms and legs.

There was a brief regret that Chris had been put in the place of meeting Wentworth's bubbly wife and two teenage daughters at this pool party—and especially at the attention, almost competitive between them, that the daughters were expending on him. But, what the hell, he thought. If it didn't bother Wentworth, it wouldn't bother him either. He had a brief tug at his conscience over that, though. He hadn't been raised to be cheating with a married man. But he suppressed that thought. It wasn't like he'd have sex with the man here in his own home, under the noses of his family.

"I don't know, Mr. Wentworth. It looks like these are the last three crab Rangoons." He'd heard his supervisor, Cathy, wafting by just a few minutes ago, saying she was on the hunt for the crab Rangoon. "They always have it here," she was telling someone else. "It's the best thing about the Wentworths' parties. I've been dreaming about it all week."

"Just indulge yourself. And then indulge me," Wentworth said. "I want to show you something in the house."

Although surprised, Chris knew what that meant, and he entered the house with Wentworth willingly.

Wentworth fucked Chris up against a wall in the master bedroom between two locked French doors, the lock to the bedroom door latched, shades drawn. The terrace with the swimming pool was just outside and the party was still going full blast. At first, Chris could clearly hear the voices of Mrs. Wentworth and the two Wentworth daughters floating out above the hubbub just on the other side of the wall, but with each deliciously cruel up-thrust of Wentworth's cock inside him, the voices receded into the general chatter.

Chris' back was against the wall and his knees were hooked on Wentworth's hips. His arms were around the older man's neck and he was moaning into the man's mouth in the lingering kiss, reveling in the feel both of the cock thrusting relentlessly up inside him and the silky sensation of Wentworth's chest hair rubbing up and down on his own smooth, nineteen-year-old chest.

Chris froze—but, strangely, Wentworth didn't, at the unsuccessful rattling of the handle of the door into the hall and the bubbly voice of Mrs. Wentworth. "You in there, Damon, honey? Why's the door locked? We're out of ice."

"Check the freezer in the garage, Dot. I know there are more bags of ice in there," Wentworth called back. He'd stopped thrusting, but was close to coming. This was the glorious release

Chris waited for with Damon; Damon came for minutes running, with multiple ejaculations. Chris had already come up Wentworth's belly, but he knew that, with Damon's specialty, he too would enjoy multiple ejaculations.

"I decided to dress," Wentworth continued in the voice pitched to carry through the bedroom door. "Took a quick shower. Locked the door so that none of the guests would wander in."

"OK, I'll check the garage freezer," the muffled voice came back. "See you in a few, I guess."

"I'll come in just a few minutes," Wentworth called back.

And come he did, within a minute, again and again and again—for a few minutes. This was Chris' favorite part of a fuck from his employer. Damon insisted on barebacking, and Chris didn't balk, because Damon came in multiple prodigious gushes that made Chris see stars and flames that spiraled down to burning embers and gave Chris the most satisfying feeling of fulfillment and comfort he had ever experienced. Wentworth came again and again in grunts and the tightening and release of his hips. Each up-thrust of the cock ended in a gush, with the slight withdrawal and repeated up-thrust and gush, like waves pounding on the beach. Chris came multiple times as well—a little sighing release with each one of Damon's spoutings. Six, seven times Damon would thrust up and release cum, until it dribbled out of Chris' hole and down his thighs.

The sensations of this were out of this world. Damon's ability was not human. Being fucked by Wentworth was like being taken by no other man—which was probably why Chris had fallen so deeply under his spell. Chris was letting loose of all of the taboos he'd been raised with by parents who had given up early on his sexual orientation and had moved on to giving him advice on how to protect himself: No older men; they would use you and leave you. No casual sex. No unprotected sex. Do not cheapen yourself by letting him call all of the shots. No married men. Don't become involved at the office.

Chris had let loose of all of these taboos, just to exchange sex that was an upward progression for sex that was a single event. Damon wasn't human; he could release spell-binding cum repeatedly for three to five minutes at a stretch, elongating the orgasm for Chris until his balls ached from his own repeated releases. When Damon fucked Chris, he was totally fucked.

Wentworth let Chris sink to the carpet with a whimpering sigh and went to take that quick shower he'd told his wife he'd already had. Alone, Chris' attention went to the sound of the party out on the terrace. He found he was listening for the voices of the wife and daughters, trying to latch onto some form of guilt from letting Wentworth have his way even in the embrace of his own family, in the bedroom he shared with his wife. And there was perhaps some vestige of guilt Chris felt, or he wouldn't have thought of it at all. At least they hadn't done it in the bed Damon shared with his wife, Chris thought. The betrayal hadn't gone that far.

He struggled to rise from the floor, picked up his red Speedo, and dabbed at his inner thighs to obliterate the globs of white cum. He wouldn't want anyone on the terrace to see that before he could reach, and dive into, the pool. A vestige of the guilt, he realized. He wasn't totally gone after all, he thought.

He felt the presence of Damon and looked up to see his employer standing there, beads of water glistening on his hairy, muscular chest, his eyes slitted as he watched Chris pat at his thighs with the red material, Damon's upcurved cock in magnificent erection again.

"Fuck 'em," Wentworth muttered in a husky voice. "I'll get back out there when I get back out there. This will only take a few minutes."

Chris was fucked in the missionary position on the side edge of the master bed. So, they *did* do it in the bed Damon shared with Dot after all. The stage of repeated ejaculation took four minutes just in itself. And Chris was left with his legs spread open, his eyes swimming in cum, and mumbling quietly to himself, a thick stain of comingled cum on the bedspread at the edge of the bed, as Damon cleaned his cock with a wet wash cloth, quickly dressed, and left the room.

This time Chris didn't think a single thought about Wentworth's family or where Wentworth had fucked him. There was something mind numbing and guilt suppressing in that cum of Wentworth's.

"Go ahead; take a handful. I'll cover for you."

"I couldn't. That would be dishonest," Chris whimpered. The whole scene was surreal to him. It was after hours at the fast-food restaurant. It had been his turn to mop the floors before leaving. He'd turned off the lights out in the dining area after mopping the kitchen floor and had shuddered in a double take as he saw the form of a man, near the windows of the dining area, backlit by the headlights of passing cars on the highway that was pretty busy even in this early morning hour.

As the man walked toward him in the murky light, seeming to materialize from a large puff of smoke, particles of ash reflecting the light from the passing cars, Chris discerned that it was Damon Wentworth. He had every right to be in his restaurant after hours. And of course he had keys to the place. He'd even said that he would appear sometime after work when Chris was left to close up and would fuck him.

The thought of Wentworth fucking him on a table top in the darkness of night, with cars passing by within thirty feet of the front windows, had aroused Chris. Any thought of Wentworth fucking him erased any other thoughts from Chris' mind and made him go hard.

Wentworth had been wrapped in a black cape and all Chris could concentrate on as the man approached was the devilish grin of his. As Wentworth drew closer, he spread the cloak open. He was naked and in gigantic erection.

Chris moaned as Wentworth came around the service counter, leaned Chris over a cash register, pulled Chris' shorts and briefs down, thrust up inside him from the rear, and, grabbing Chris' wrists, spread his arms along the counter and trapped him there, as he nuzzled Chris' neck with his lips and fucked him with his cock.

As Chris writhed under his employer, the cash register made a dinging noise and popped open. It was full of cash. The registers were supposed to be cleared out by the manager at night, with the money deposited in the night machine of a nearby bank.

As Wentworth's thrusts came quicker and went deeper, Chris writhed more under him, and bills started flipping out of the cash register and onto the floor.

"Shouldn't we . . . ?" Chris murmured with a gasp.

"There's no money in the registers," Damon answered, with a laugh. "It will have all been taken to the bank. So help yourself. Go ahead; take a handful. It doesn't really exist. I'll cover for you."

"I couldn't. That would be dishonest," Chris whimpered. But then he cried out, "Oh, my God. Shit. Yes!" as Damon's first ejaculation exploded inside him, cum spurting up into his intestines. Damon reared back and then thrust and ejaculated again. And again. And again. Waves and waves of prodigious spoutings of cum, making Chris come again and again, as well.

Blinding flames and heat seared through Chris' brain. He was swimming through the hot lava of Damon's erupting cum. Until he found himself on the floor of the restaurant, behind the counter, his back against the service counter. He was alone, whimpering, sitting in a slick of cum on the floor—Damon's and his. Light from the passing headlights of cars was flickering off the silver metal of the drink machines in front of him. Money was strewn over his lap. He looked up, above his head. The cash register drawer appeared to be closed.

Struggling up from the floor, his hands busy gathering up the bills and sifting them into one large bundle, Chris' eyes verified that the drawer was closed and wouldn't open without a key, which he didn't have, after hours. He laid the bills on the counter and, with shaking hands, tried to open the drawer anyway. But he couldn't. He stood there for a moment, in thought. He could get into the office. Maybe there were night deposit envelopes and slips there. He'd take this money to the bank himself.

His hands, still shaky, he counted the money. More than three-hundred dollars.

Yes, there were envelopes and slips in the office. He filled a slip out and inserted the money in the envelope. He hadn't deposited money at the bank himself, but he'd gone along with Cathy a few times, to give her some protection, when she made a deposit. He could do this.

As he got to the door of the restaurant, he remembered the mess from the sex on the floor below the cash register. He'd put the money in his glove compartment and come back to swab the floor there.

When he opened the passenger door to the car, he gave off an "Oofff," as he was pushed down onto his belly on the passenger seat. The envelope skitted onto the driver's seat, split open, and the bills scattered out.

Both of them were covered by the undulating black cloak, as Damon, first, fucked Chris from behind, and then, as the ejaculations started, turned the young man on his back and covered him, rubbing his hairy chest up and down on Chris'. Damon grabbed handfulls of money and stuffed them in Chris' mouth. He then grabbed Chris' wrists and stretched the young man's arms over his head as he ejaculated again and again. Each time Damon spouted he growled, "Spend the money. Spend the money."

When Chris came too, Damon was gone. He gathered up the bills, like a zombie, having no idea where they'd come from—or how or why. He bought a new flat screen TV the next day, and if anyone had asked him where he got the money for it—although no one did—he wouldn't have had the vaguest notion where it had come from.

* * * *

"I'm going to the men's room. After I leave, you take a circuitous route to the exit, and I'll meet you in the car."

Damon and Chris had stopped at an expensive—and crowded—restaurant en route to a trailer out in the wilderness on the banks of a lake, where Damon was going to attend a poker party. He'd made quite clear that Chris was along to serve the men—and not just with pretzels and cheese dip. Chris took it as some sort of test of wills. Damon said he'd give Chris a good fuck himself afterward—if Chris pleased the other men.

But Chris saw this, the restaurant stop, as a test of wills too. He didn't know what it was a test for. Just in his more introspective moments—when he wasn't thinking of what Damon could do to him—what he wanted Damon doing to him—he knew that something inside him, his integrity or something, was slipping away from him and that there was some sort of methodical move going on in this regard. He sensed a downward spiral, but he didn't have the will to either arrest the sinking feeling or examine it in any depth.

The bill had arrived. Damon had taken a look at it and closed the pad, not making a move to reach for his wallet—although if you viewed the gesture from afar, you might have supposed Damon had put a credit card inside.

Chris didn't say anything when Damon gave his instructions, but he gave Damon a searching "Are we really going to do this?" look. He watched Damon walk away toward the restrooms. Then Chris stood, opened the check pad to see how much the meal had been, and felt his hand go to his own back pocket. But he also felt the eyes boring into him and lifted his face to see that Damon was watching him from across the crowded dining room.

With a sigh, Chris closed the pad and turned and walked around the periphery of the dining area and through another one of the dining rooms before approaching the door to the street and, after a slight hesitancy, exiting the restaurant.

He had done it—stiffed the restaurant for his meal. A couple of weeks ago he wouldn't have imagined in his wildest dreams that he would do such a thing. He gave brief thought to what he'd done and to why, but before he could muster much at all in thought, he looked up, and there was Damon by the car, smiling his devilish smile, his eyes looking intently at Chris. When he reached the car, he pressed Chris' body up against the side of the car with his and gave him a deep kiss. He had one hand caressing and patting Chris' head like Chris was a good dog who had just passed an obedience test. The other hand was groping Chris' crotch.

"You drive and take the car over to the far end of the parking lot there, in the shadows," Damon instructed in a husky voice.

In the shadows of the restaurant's lot, Damon pulled Chris, trouserless, over to straddle his lap on the passenger seat and gave Chris the glorious, numbing three-minute ejaculation that kept Chris fully under his control.

In the trailer out on the shore of the wooded lake, Chris lay under a succession of randy men at Damon's direction, on a studio bed adjacent to the poker table, through the early hours of the morning. The order of the men and duration of their dicks moving inside Chris' ass was dictated by their willingness to fold their hands in standoffs with Damon at the table. Over a four-hour period, Chris earned well over a thousand dollars for Damon—or so he thought.

Later in the morning, when, laying between Chris' legs, Damon had pumped the mesmerizing nectar of his ejaculate inside Chris for nearly five continuous minutes and Chris was laying, spread-eagled, moaning slightly, his mouth agape, and panting shallowly in ecstasy, Damon stuffed the poker winnings in Chris' mouth, muttered, "Now you are a whore," and was gone.

It didn't occur to Chris to think in any depth about having, for the first time in his life, let multiple men fuck him in succession or that he had prostituted himself by accepting money for having done so, as long as the scent and memory of Damon were in the room. Sometime later there was a bit of a twinge, but he pushed it to the back of his mind immediately. He knew that Damon would disapprove and say he was weak if he allowed himself to think about it.

* * * *

If Damon hadn't been fucking Chris when he laid out the plan, Chris might have realized how wrong it was. But Damon's possession of and victory over Chris was almost totally complete. Damon had just given Chris that devilish grin of his while he was pumping him, and Chris didn't even think to ask why it was necessary for the two of them to burglarize a jewelry store at night. Chris didn't need any jewelry and Damon was so obviously rich that he could afford to buy his wife whatever she wanted and wouldn't miss whatever if cost.

But there they were, leaning over the smashed glass of a jewelry display case in a dark store, Damon covering Chris' back, fucking him and releasing spurt after spurt of ejaculate. Chris' arms were pushed into the display case and he was fisting diamond bracelets as he moaned at the prolonged taking.

133

Chris was so wrapped up in the fucking that he barely noticed the ringing of the store's alarm; the approaching sirens; or, as Damon leaned his mouth closely to Chris' ear to deliver one last statement with a satanic laugh, the swirl of the red lights on the ceiling of the darkened display room.

"You are totally fucked and completely mine now," Damon said, as he pulled out of Chris' ass and off his back and disappeared in the swirl of a black cape and a puff of smoked. As he disappeared, leaving Chris draped over the display case and fisting diamond bracelets, the front door of the store gave way and the policemen, guns drawn, began to circle around the room.

Only now, with the sensation that Damon's controlling presence had been totally withdrawn—even though he was "down there" and watching, with that devilish grin of his—did the clouds start to clear away from Chris' muddled mind and he began to see the depths to which his life had spiraled.

~

About the Author

Habu is one of the pen names of a former supersonic spy jet pilot, intelligence agent, male model, movie actor, and diplomat. A wild youth in South East Asia was spent enjoying whatever sexual opportunities came his way, and much of his gay male writing is about recalling incidents from those days and inventing ones he'd perhaps have liked to experience. He now leads a very quiet and ordinary happily married family life.

An American, he is a published mainstream novelist and short story writer under another name and in another dimension of his life. He has written or cowritten (with Sabb) approaching 1,000 published short stories and over 100 published erotica e-books, primarily of gay fiction but also memoir, straight fiction and ménage fiction. His hand and creative writing can be seen in stories and books by habu, sr71plt, Dirk Hessian, Shabbu, and Stephen Kessel—among unrevealed others that might surprise readers. The fictionalized GM memoir *Flying High, Diving Deep* is loosely based on his life experiences. He can be found at the adults only gay male site www.BarbarianSpy.com, which he shares with Sabb and Dirk Hessian.

Our authors always like to receive feedback, and appreciate it when readers post reviews at distributors and other sites.

 *BarbarianSpy*

FOR LITERARY HEAT

Not all books listed below may currently be on release.
* indicates the book is available in paperback and e-book.

BOOKS BY DIRK HESSIAN
Xtreme Erotica
The King's Men
Shores of Tripoli
Prophecy of Noto
Pretender's Fate
General Erotica/Romance
Fire Down the Valley*
Constantinople*
The Beautiful Way*
Blue and Gray
Colonel's Treasure
Beginning of Time
Labyrinth
BOOKS BY HABU
Gay Erotica
Memoir Faction
Flying High, Diving Deep*
Xtreme Erotica
Silas' Choice*
Last Call
Choke Hold
Apyko: The Greek Pimp
Visits of the Schlange
Second Coming: Emile La Cour Unleashed
Vortex: Sacrificed by Curiosity*
Dark Angel Sounding *(in e-book & included in Sounding:Ultimate Control Paperback)**
Sounding: Ultimate Control (*Print Only*)*
Sounding Five *(in e-book & included in Sounding:Ultimate Control paperback)**

Romance
Sugar n Spice Christmas
Tank 'n Bull
Sail to the Sun
War Letters
Ravens Roost
Caribbean Cruise Top to Bottom
Arena Stage
Trading Partners (Valentine's Day)
Friday Nights with Lenny (Christmas Romance)
Snowy, Snowy Nights (Christmas Romance)
Four Coins
Lower Than the Heart (Valentine's Day)
Brambleton
Gotta Keep Trying
Finding Amnad
Platres Conclave
Other Novels/Novellas
Journey Through Abilene
Harmony and Dissonance
Stallion Station
Racing With the Devil (espionage suspense)
Cruising Gigolo (bisexual)
Prepared in Cape Verdi
Gilded Cage
House on Park
Anything for Ambition
Dance of the Ravishers
Hard Knocks U*
My Neighbor's Spa*
Man's Man: Tales of a High Priced Gay Hooker*
Trip Money
The Indian Doctor
Sailorboy
Home to Fire Island
Murder Mysteries
Death on a Ping Pong Table
Clint Folsom Mysteries Compendium Volume 1*

Death to Blonds - Stolen Judgment (Clint Folsom Mystery)*
Clint Folsom Mysteries Compendium Volume 2*
Gay Erotica Anthologies
DevilMENt*
Silas' Choices*
Stallion Station (A Novella in Parts)
Eleven to the Dogs*
Fifty Seventy*
Spy Tails 001*
Spy Tails 002*
Doubled*
Doubled Again*
Tails in the Tropics*
Tails in the Med*
Tails in the West*
Rough Riders*
Grab Bag 1*
Grab Bag 2*
Grab Bag 3*
Grab Bag 4*
Grab Bag 5*
Grab Bag 6*
Beyond the Beaded Curtain*
Habu's Christmas Balls
The Sporting Life*
Fetish Galore!*
Literary Gay Erotica
Cairo Surrender*
The Handyman*
Homeward Bound
Journey to Mirage*
Bi-Sexual/Menage Erotica
Death on a Pool Table
Cruising Gigolo
13 Ways for Halloween
Luther*
The Indian Prince

Literary GLBT Fiction
Summer of Denial
BOOKS BY SHABBU
Velvet Interrogation
Finding Jason
Dirty Pool
Operation Black Jade
Cigars!*
Angel in the Barn
Gayly Complicated*
Despoiling David
The Tree of Idleness*
I Met a Man
Rough Road to Happiness
BOOKS BY SABB
Hiring in Hollywood
The Legend of Holleystone Grange
Surprise Encounters
She is He
Wrong Man
Loyal to his King
Barbarian Tales - Book One - Traveler's Tales*
Barbarian Tales - Book Two - Journeys Begin*
Barbarian Tales - Book Three - The Inheritance*
Barbarian Tales - Book Four - Road to Persepolis*